Indigo Travelers
And the
Lost Murdoc Princess
Book 3

Indigo Traveler Series

By Merri Halma

Merri Halma (USA)
This edition published in 2018 by Dreaming Lizard (USA)
Copyright © Merri Halma Dreaming Lizard 2018
Cover Art © Cynthia Martinez
Editing © Blazing Butterfly Edit 2018
Interior Format & Design © Blazing Butterfly Edit 2018

ISBN 13:978-0692081358
ISBN 10: 0692081356

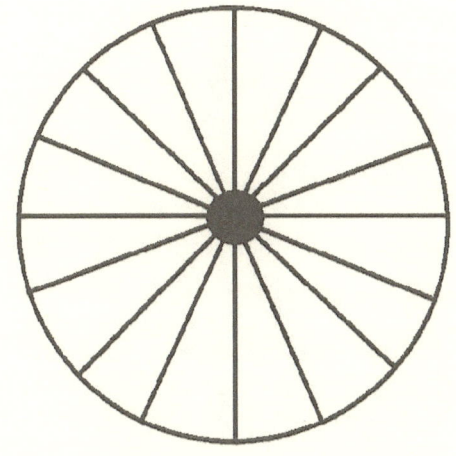

All Paths lead to Albagoth
All are equal
Albagoth leads all within
The Teachings of Albagoth

Merri Halma

Summary of Indigo Travelers and the Keys to the Shadowlands

Sarah ran and ran until she couldn't run anymore. She reached a tree with long weeping branches and touched it. "What am I doing? I just admitted to my friends that I'm an alien. I always thought I was human. My parents lied to me. I saw my birth certificate and it says I am their daughter, but that's another lie." She turned around, leaning her bottom against the trunk.

"Friends, true friends, will not turn their back on you. You turned your back on them, leaving them to fight among themselves. They're tearing each other apart."

Sarah looked around, "Who said that?"

"I did. I'm Raindom. I mourn for all that was lost when my seed blew into this land. I am a banyan tree, also known as a wisdom tree. There's no one to impart my wisdom to here. No one listens. You, daughter of Murdoc, will understand," the tree spoke.

"Daughter of Murdoc? What do you mean?" Sarah turned to face the tree.

"Your people are called Murdoc. Yet you are part human and they knew you would be much taller than they are. You are better able to suit the world you are being raised on."

Raindom let out an amused chuckled. "Sarah, you are born of two paths – one path seeks to live with nature and respect the land they live on that feeds them. The other path follows the one that died and came back from the dead to lead them to promised land. You need to forge your own path. You are the key, dear child. You are the key to bring light to this dark world."

As Sarah reflected on what Rain told her, she heard the tree's unspoken words, *The world you are from is divided into three main spiritual parts. All one people, two of the paths deny they are related to the third and they deny*

Albagoth. The Lost Princess will unite them. Sarah, you are the key. Anansi will lead the way.

Chapter 1

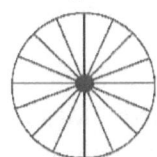

The solar winds tossed Geoffrey, the griffin, around like a rag doll as meteors flew past at high speed. As two wormholes opened, Geoffrey struggled to take the one on the left, knowing that would lead to the World of Nampa. Yet between dodging the meteors and going against solar winds, Geoffrey was blown down the right one shouting to his passengers, "Hang on tight!" as they went into an uncontrollable tailspin.

Sarah closed her eyes. Visions of large hairy spiders crawling around toward Sarah swam behind her closed eyes. As the spiders neared her, she noticed each spider had a distinct marking on its forehead. *Go away, spiders, ewww! You scare me.*

A spider with a tattoo of a circle with many divisions spoke, "We are your protectors, friends and guides. One of us will be your companion for now on. Trust us to lead you to your birth father."

Eww! Go away!

The more the solar winds tossed them around, the more Sarah struggled to stay on. She dared to open her eyes, only to see the black vacuum of space- dotted with stars- down to the world below zoom closer in view, like getting vertigo from looking down from the top floor of a high-rise building. Her stomach dropped. She sensed the boys also felt like they didn't have control of what was happening to them.

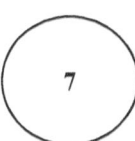

Sarah noticed Milo held tight to the feathers on Geoffrey's neck.

She closed her eyes to shut out the vertigo, the spiders came into her vision once again, *We're your friends, Sarah. You can trust us,* she felt them telling her. *No, you can't be my friends! I hate you, you freaky creepy crawlers! Go away!*

The visions were so real, Sarah could feel the stiff hairs on their legs and pointy front toes of each one on her skin. She let go of Milo's waist with one hand to sap them off and scratch herself. Vertigo, mixed with slapping the spiders in her visions, caused her to lose her balance. She fell.

Xander reached out a hand to grab her, but Sarah pulled away causing Xander to lean over further to grab her left foot. However, the momentum of Sarah's fall pulled him off, too. He managed to pull himself hand over hand down her body till he reached her left forearm.

Sarah soared fast; she remembered the black paracord bracelet. Xander reached for her hand that the bracelet was on, just as she was reaching across her body to it. She felt Xander's thoughts beseeching Albagoth for help.

Sarah pull the cord on the black bracelet, *we need protective suits* she told the bracelet which immediately transformed into a large bubble around them.

Sarah saw in her mind's eye two hearts merging into one large unit. The image warmed her whole being, until it occurred to her that it meant they could become an item. *I'm not ready for a relationship*, she mused. *At least the spiders went away.* As they entered the world's atmosphere, where they could now see the land below, she asked the bracelet to transform into a parachute now

"Grab one end, Xander!" Sarah yelled over the rushing wind. It was like jumping into the eye of a hurricane, spinning them around rapidly. Xander took the other end of the parachute. She glanced at him in a reassuring that they would be okay so that he would let go of the vise like grip on her arm. Sarah could sense Xander was thanking the Albagoth for this parachute.

From above, they could see desert, with sparse trees and bushes. The sky was dark, and they could hear some type of sharp particles hitting the outside of the parachute and protective barrier. Sarah and Xander exchanged puzzled expressions, wondering what kind of world they were entering.

Once they landed, Sarah asked the paracord bracelet to form a two -room tent around them to protect them from the outside weather. Once it did so, she examined it and was satisfied with the shape and size. There was a divider between the two rooms, that allowed them could see each other. Each room had a plastic window. However, Xander's room had a door which led to the outside.

Scanning the ground, Sarah could see the glass shards that fell and crunched underneath them. The ground didn't feel wet, as such, but it reminded her of someone breaking a whole shipment of crystal plates.

Sarah looked down at her crumpled clothes and started straightening her black trousers and fussing with her army boots. Sensing his intense gaze drilling a hole in the back of her head, Sarah turned to meet his eye straight on. A deep anger and outrage rose from her belly.

"You want to know where I got this and how it works, right?" Sarah asked, snidely.

"Well, yeah – sort of. I mean, you're not Hermione, are you?" Xander countered, sounding gruff.

"No, but she is very cool. She's smart, tough, and she knows how to put Ron and Harry in their place when she has to." Sarah smiled. Breaking the gaze, she looked out of the plastic window of the tent. "Healer Jephra gave it to me before we left. He said all I had to do was pull the cord in the middle while thinking of what I need at the time. So, when we fell off, I pulled the cord while envisioning a protective suit around us, so we wouldn't explode in the vacuum of space. Once we entered the atmosphere, I asked it to change into a parachute so slow our descent to the ground. As we neared the land, I changed the thought to a dwelling for two."

"Why did he give it to you and not to me?" Xander asked, his voice sounding annoyed.

Sarah shrugged her shoulders, "Not sure. Maybe he sensed something would happen to us on the way home. And maybe he felt I had an ability to create what we needed to keep us safe. After all, *I* am the one that opened up the Shadowlands, so the Crow Judges could come in and capture that Daphne Raven Judge of the Shadowlands who was making trouble for everyone."

"You don't have to rub that in, you know!" Xander snarled.

Narrowing her eyes, Sarah sought to see underneath Xander's anger, and sharp tone. She saw his hurt feelings, confusing imagery of how he was felt entitled to be the hero of Shadowlands and she displaced him. Now, he didn't know who he was or what his role in the whole journey. He also believed she was to be the weak one, but again, she showed him she can handle herself. He couldn't admit his feelings or admit his ego is bruised. Sarah let out a small laugh, shaking her head, thinking he's a typical guy.

"What's so funny?" Xander accused.

"Guys! You are. You think you're so tough, wise and the only one who can solve problems or even see through others. You didn't have to try to keep me on Geoffrey, Xander! But no – you had to try to pull me up and you fell off with me. Ever think I was meant to be here on this world without you?" Sarah shouted. Her gaze steadfast, her blue eyes turned to ice, wishing she could punch him.

Sarah saw her words hit Xander with full force, stumbling a bit. He slumped his shoulders as he turned around. *Maybe I was too hard on him,* Sarah wondered, feeling bad she yelled him. *But look at him sulk. That just makes him look so cute and vulnerable. Yet, he chose to try to save me when I didn't ask for it. Perhaps he needs to hear the truth.*

Sarah took her eyes off Xander and thought about how they were going to sleep. Pushing her long blond hair out of her eyes, she surveyed the surroundings. They didn't have blankets and she didn't have Milo's ability to wish for them and pillows. She sighed, deciding they could get by without them. She sat down, choosing to listen to the rain or whatever that was that falling from the sky outside. The steady, sharp hard stuff hitting the tent reminded Sarah of hail back home. She was thankful the tent could adapt to the climates. Yet the sharp *ting* or *ping* as it hit the fabric sounded more like stones or glass shards hitting aluminum. The rhythm lulled Sarah into a semi-meditative state. She closed her eyes, trying to center herself on imagining what they would encounter here.

Her inner vision of many paths divided by mazes of trees and shrubs, and three different villages who vied for rule was abruptly interrupted as she felt Xander glaring at her from the other room. She looked at him.

"Fine! You want to be alone, I will leave you alone!" Xander shouted as he started to leave through the door.

What a baby, Sarah thought to herself. *He's cute when he's angry. He's also intelligent, but he's such a whiner. I should just tell him to go.*

"Don't go out there in this – this—whatever it is that is falling. It sounds like it could really hurt you," Sarah warned. *Uh, why did I say that? I meant to tell him not to let the door hit him on the backside on his way out.*

Xander lowered his head; Sarah was sure she could see steam coming out of his ears and nose as he plopped down on the moist ground that was scattered with sharp shards that fell. They were still falling outside the tent. She watched as he picked up one of the pieces to examine it. She stood up and walked over to look at it over his shoulder.

"What does it feel like?" Sarah asked, noticing the sparkles coming from it.

"It feels like a type of glass, and yet burns my fingertips. It must be kind of an acid-based crystal or something." He tossed it down. Scanning the ground beneath him, he said, "I wish I had a magic wand to make a softer place to sit and to clear this small room," he said.

"I wish I had one, too, so we could have soft beds, pillows and warm blankets," Sarah added. They both let out a half chuckle, their eyes met. Sarah felt a stab in her heart as a desire to embrace him over took her, but she fought it. *This isn't the time or place for it,* she told herself. She glanced away from his eyes, and back. She noticed Xander's face flushed a bit, too. He stared back at the shard in his fingers and then let go. She patted his shoulder, "Night, Xander," she said, turning to walk self-consciously back to her side of the tent. Once there, she sat down and looked back.

Sarah watched Xander yawn and stretch his arms and legs. He did the best he could to sweep the ground below him and laid down. Soon, she heard him snoring. She averted her gaze, choosing to look out the window and sighed.

Albagoth, Xander says he trusts you. I've only met you once but understand you have had numerous discussions with him since his first trip to Curá. I was wondering if you could send a guide or send me a dream so I knew what this world is and what to expect. She yawned. *Not sure I want to sleep if it means more dreams of spiders.* She laid down as her eyelid began to feel too heavy to keep open.

Sarah saw herself walking into a clearing that was surrounded by trees. In the middle was a symbol of a large circle with many divisions leading to a smaller circle. A voice spoke to her, "All paths lead to me, Sarah. All paths are equal. Some of the villagers you will meet think they are more equal than others. Only one group know the truth that are handed down in a book only the Crow Judges back on Curá are taught from childhood. Come into the circle and I will tell you more.

Sarah walked into the circle, knowing the voice that spoke was Albagoth, but didn't know how she knew. This is a dream. A vision, she thought. Xander told me about visions. Why am I having this one?

This world, Sarah, is your home. You are the one to unite the divisions and show the rival paths they are all the same. They are all Murdocs, even though they follow different beliefs. I bless them all. Part of me is within each one, even though they refuse to recognize me. Follow the Anansi to the Albaohma Davineh.

Suddenly there before her was a large spider, with his eight eyes staring at her, smiling. *"We're called Anansi, Sarah. We're here to guide you to your home and so you can meet with your father, Davineh. I'm Nickoli."*

Sarah stared at the creature. It had the symbol of the circle with many sections on its forehead. The same one she saw in the field. The same symbol she'd been seeing in dreams for two weeks back home.

"I don't care who you are! I'm not going anywhere with you! Go away!" she shouted out loud, still asleep. The Anansi urged her to trust him. She continued to tell it to go away, saying she hated spiders. It started shaking her violently, getting angry that she wasn't listening to him. She balled up her fist and swung as hard as she could, "I said leave me alone!"

Sarah's fist connected with flesh and bone, jarring her awake. She sat up to see Xander sitting on the other side of her room, rubbing his jaw.

"What are you doing on my side?" Sarah shouted, not bothering to find out if he was okay.

"You were having a bad dream. I was trying to let you know you were alright and there were no spiders here," Xander answered in his defense. "Where did you learn to slug like that? You could've broke my jaw!"

"I have an older brother that picked on me. I had to learn to defend myself."

Xander drew his eyebrows down, looking quite cross. "You could've broke my jaw."

"You could've ignored me and went back to sleep," Sarah fired back.

Xander shook his head. He let out a slow breath and then put his hand down and stood up, "Not sure why you're so angry with me. I'm only trying to look out for you."

"How are you trying to look out for me? It seems like you are acting like a spoiled brat because you weren't the one to open the Shadowlands and you're hurt that Jephra didn't give you the black bracelet. You think you're so entitled, Alexander Veh! Has it ever occurred to you that Milo and I are also Indigo teens and perhaps have the same abilities to help others?" She thought again, realizing their abilities are different. "I mean, I am capable of protecting myself and don't need you to watch out for me like I'm a helpless child. After all, I was the one fighting Butch when you couldn't stand up for yourself."

Xander turned his back to her, hanging his head. "I'm not that helpless kid anymore, Sarah. Now, I know how to fight for myself and I'm always reading that girls are weaker and need us boys to protect them. I just thought I was doing the right thing," he said slowly.

"I've never been a helpless and weak female. You should have realized that about me a long time ago!"

Xander slumped his shoulders. "I guess you're right. I never know what the right thing is anymore," he uttered in a weak voice as he walked back to his side of the tent.

Sarah watched him go, feeling sorry she yelled at him. She glanced out the window and heard birds chirping. She realized whatever it was that was falling stopped and it was quiet. Except for the birds. She reflected on her words to her friend. *Maybe I shouldn't have been so harsh to him.* Her stomach rumbled. Then she heard Xander's stomach rumble from the next room.

"Hey, do you hear that?" he called.

"No. What do you hear?" she answered.

"It's quiet. I mean the rain shards stopped. Let's put the tent away and go look for some food. Or a village where we can find some food," Xander suggested.

"That sounds good to me," she said, standing and going to the corner looking for the little cord. She walked out and around the tent. Xander followed. After she found it, she took it between her thumb and forefinger, *Thank you for the parachute and the tent. Please return to bracelet,* she thought. The tent folded itself up and drifted down into her open palm as the black bracelet. She put it back on her left wrist.

"Let's go," she said, leading him down the path.

"How do you know where to go? And do you know where we are?" Xander said, running to catch up to her.

"I don't know where we are. Nor do I know which direction to go, it just makes sense to walk this way," Sarah replied.

Xander shrugged his shoulders, pausing in his tracks. Sarah wasn't slowing down for him. He ran to catch up.

"Look, we need to find Milo and Geoffrey. It's important to find them before we all get further separated. Besides, I had dreamt my mom found Milo's parents. I need to tell him," Xander offered.

"We will find them. First, we need to find out what world this is and find some food. Maybe we can find some rabbit or something and twigs to make a fire," Sarah replied.

15

"We need to find out where we are, too," Xander ventured.

"We will," Sarah replied, though she wasn't so sure why she felt so confident.

They walked in silence.

The trees appeared to bow when they saw Sarah. Birds were tweeting, and flitted around, but paused to watch them. Little creatures scurried out from under the bushes, to watch them pass. One little mouse waved a paw.

"Hello," Sarah answered. "Can you speak?"

The mouse shook its head as if to say no, turned around and ran back under the bush.

Sarah sighed. Up ahead, she thought she saw the bush and trees moving to one side, rotating as if they were tired of standing in one position and needed to move to wake up their limbs.

Off to the left, she thought she saw a clearing. It reminded her of her dream. She shook her head to jar the memory.

"It's only a dream," she muttered half out loud.

"Dreams are important. My mom says to pay attention to them," Xander offered. "Tell me about it."

"No, it's too personal," she said. Her mind swirled between anger mixed with sadness at being raised with humans, believing she was human, yet finding out she was truly an alien, like her brother, Jarrod, used to taunt about. *Why didn't my parents tell me about being from a different world? About being adopted?*

A bright light, like the sun light bouncing off an object in the distance catching Sarah's eye, so she veered off the path. Xander followed her without questioning. The closer she got to it, she could see a statue of three people. It appeared one of them was a man who had been bound to a tree, but the bindings broke.

In the center of the meadow stood a statue of a man tied upside down to a large tree. Some of the ropes had frayed and snapped, causing him to fall head first down to a cloaked figure who was inside a hole. It looked like the cloaked figure was pulling the first man down the hole. Beside the tree, was a woman kneeling, reaching with one hand for the falling man and the other hand for the cloaked figure as if she was trying to prevent the first from being pulled below.

Sarah walked around the statues looking for a plaque or something that would explain what the statue represented. Xander followed her, puzzled. She found it.

It stated: *The Wraith pulling our Savior into the Black Hole after he failed to convert the evil Murdocs to our blessed path. Our Blessed Mother crying cleansing tears to stop the Foolishness.*

Sarah scowled, and muttered, "Murdocs are not evil. Whoever it is that is depicted here are the evil ones. Who are they to pass judgment on people who are smaller than they are?"

"How do you know?" Xander cocked his head to one side, considering her words, though he barely heard them.

"I can't explain how I know. I just know," she hissed.

Xander shook his head back and forth, "I don't understand what you're upset about. We know nothing of these Murdocs."

He paused, thinking back.

"I remember one time a little man appeared to me riding a spider. I believe he called himself a Murdoc." His head went back, realizing, "Sarah, your concerns about being adopted and dreams of spiders are connected. Maybe you are part Murdoc and you will find your birth people."

"You know nothing, Alexander Veh!" Sarah hissed. "I will not discuss my personal problems with you!"

Sarah abruptly turned around and started to stomp off, then paused, admitting it bothered her that Xander tried to understand her concerns about being adopted. Her thoughts changed swiftly as it dawned on her that the statue could be a clue to her dreams and spider visions; it could have the answers she need, or it could bring up more questions.

She addressed it, "Okay, Fallen Savior and Wraith, explain to me why you two hate the Murdocs so much. What have they done to you?" She held a hand out as she walked closer. "Show me your lives."

Xander watched, wide-eyed, not sure what she was doing. Inside, he knew he better close his mouth and watch.

Before Sarah's eyes, the statue began to glow from within and the figures began moving, the Fallen Savior straightened himself up, the Mother figure pulled him over and the Wraith figure climbed out of the Black Hole. The tree opened, the figures walked in, turned to her and beckoned her to follow.

Once through, the land looked bright, shimmering with trees and rich shrubs and paths in every direction. She saw small people, some riding spiders and others walking beside the spiders, some of them were busy gathering edible roots, others watering the plants, or pulling what she guessed were weeds, and others were gathering twigs. Sarah guessed the twigs would be used to build a fire. Those gathering twigs and branches, piled them on top of their spiders to carry back the main meeting place. Sarah followed the statue people, though the two men figures gradually reduced in size and the woman also shrunk, losing her bronze appearance. She was greeted by a spider, with a drawing of a strong tree merging two different paths. Sarah walked in front, turned around to see the young woman, noticing she had a different drawing on her forehead. Her drawing depicted a broken tree with two saplings walking down two different paths.

Sarah noticed the woman appeared to be about her age, fifteen, with an oval face framed by long blond hair pulled back with a leather string tied around it. Her tan skin glowed from walking helping gather the twigs. The whole village was buzzing with activities.

"He's coming back today," she told her spider. "The feast will be perfect for him to celebrate his new status as the new Albaohman."

"Princess Miriam, you know Tomás will not be staying here. As I understand it, he is still traveling to other worlds, learning their spiritual stories and guiding travelers on their journeys. He is still an apprentice with your father, King Caden," her spider said.

"Yes, I know. But things will change. You'll see. Once Tomás sees how much I've grown and matured, he will want to stay here and settle down with me. We will give him an Anansi to travel with him who will also help guide others. And we will give him an engraving, too, that represents his calling in this life. Albagoth has shown me," Miriam's eyes twinkled. Sarah recognized the daydream of a young teen lost in love.

"I don't know, Princess. He's human and your father and mother might not allow the union. You have your own mission to heal. You can change your engraving as long as you change your inner desires."

"You're a spoiled sport, Anony. Father loves Tomás, why wouldn't he accept him as my chosen? And no one knows what my engraving means. That's why I'm spending my free time working with the spruce tree down outside the village to discern what it means."

Anony rolled four of her eyes at the same time she lifted a leg, with the tiny paw upward, "Please give me strength, Albagoth, to guide the princess." She turned back to her partner, "We've been over this before. Your engraving says you will have offspring that will break off from our Murdoc way and each will forge two different paths. That can't be good, your highness. That spells trouble for our way of life."

"Perhaps not. Perhaps you all will find a way to accept my offspring."

19

Sarah saw the scenes rushing forward like someone pushed fast forward on the DVD player. The scene stopped, zeroing in on a man, Sarah guessed was Tomás, sitting on a rock with many of the Murdoc children, teens, and adults gathered around him. Miriam sat in front of the group, at the bard's feet, and her parents—the king and queen—dressed in similar tunics and leggings wearing crowns made of flowers and herbs around their heads, sitting off to the side on smaller boulders. The spiders, which Sarah now realized were called Anansi, were also in the group near their partners. Sarah listened as Tomás spoke of the creation story, god from the human world disguising himself as human in order to seduce a beautiful young woman. They had many children, which became demigods and heroes. There was another story of a man who was the son of a god who was hung for teaching about his father in heaven, as they called it. Miriam loved that story, in awe of how wonderful it would be to give birth to children who were part god.

The scene faded and when it came back, Miriam was walking with a man, she guessed was Tomás, hand in hand. She heard them discussing the mythos stories. Tomás how the creative spirit lies within each person. He reminded her Albagoth teaches each person to go within to connect with that. Then, Miriam agreed, but deep inside, Sarah could see she still harbored a belief those stories had a seed of truth.

She changed the topic, saying she loved him and he said it back. They turned to each other and started kissing. The scene made her think of Xander, briefly wishing she could kiss him, but changed her mind. She couldn't admit that to him or anyone else now. For now, she had to keep him guessing.

The scene changed to show Miriam, some years later with twin boys. Tomás stood talking with her as they watched the boys play. "I admit to being their father, but I cannot stay and help you raise them, Miriam. My calling is to travel to other worlds, learning their stories and sharing the wisdom of Albagoth, without asking any of them to convert. I also guide travelers to strange worlds as they search for meaning. Not everyone will see all paths leading to Albagoth and the genderless spirit has taught me to accept each one where he is. When I come back to Wayla, I will spend time with the boys and teach them, too. For now, they have the Albaohmen, and your parents to guide them. You, must guide them in the ways of your spiritual understanding."

Miriam shook her head, "No, I will not."

Tomás knitted his brow and then glanced around, "I don't understand why not." He continued to look around and started pacing around the outside, looking under shrubs, "Where's Anony? I haven't seen her for a couple days."

"We had a fight and I sent her away. She's been united with another budding young woman who has the same path and calling as her."

"And you weren't given another Anansi?" Tomás raised an eyebrow.

"Let's just say I have chosen to raise my boys away from the Murdoc way. We will forge our own path."

Tomás, tall with dark hair, and skin that looked like a cross between white and brown, raised a shoulder considering her words. Sarah could see part of him was at odds with what she said, because it meant her boys would deviate from the path their mother was raised in. It also meant she had to abdicate her inheritance to the throne. He wondered what that would mean for the future of the monarchy. The Murdocs, even though they had a king and queen, weren't above the others. They worked alongside others and welcomed votes on what they needed to do as a society.

Gradually the scene changed one more time; she saw the twins, older, now about ten years old, walking toward the

Murdoc Village. "You can't go in there, Marshall," the smaller twin with light-colored hair and a muddy complexion, say to the taller twin with jet black hair and white complexion.

"I can do what I want. Besides, just because Mother says not to bother them, I'm fascinated in them. They say the Nameless one is genderless and couldn't have fathered us. One even said our father is human," Marshall mused. He laughed. "Can you imagine having a human here on Wayla? According the stories Tomás says, they're stupid and fall for anything so dumb. I mean, wouldn't it be silly to have a god who disguises himself as a human?"

"Mother says the Nameless One is a god and he appeared to her as what he was. Wouldn't that mean Mother was dumb for falling in love with him?" the smaller one, Sarah learned his name was Ira, said.

"No, not really. She was young. What angers me more is that the Nameless One refuses to visit us again and claim us the way he did in that other story of the man who was hung from a tree. Come on, Ira, come with me."

"No, I better not. I'm busy trying to form my own path, like Mother wants us to do."

"How are you going to do that?" Marshall asked.

"I spend time by the water, practicing using my magic to dig holes. I want to punish the Murdocs for kicking Mom out of the village and rejecting us. They made her give up her right to the throne. As I chant spells to create the holes, I imagine demons like Tomás describes. I call it the Black Hole. What are you doing with your path?"

Marshall shrugged, glanced away, narrowing his eyes. "I'm studying the Murdocs. They have some good ideas, but they're misguided. If the god they believe in is all good, and came down once to meet with Mother, then he can come down again. Everything has gender. Therefore, this being must be either male or female. I choose to do good and do what I can to influence them to come to my way of thinking. Maybe we all are the Nameless One's children by adoption. Maybe I can be the one to lead others to see him as a father figure. And not to worship trees or pray to them."

Then the scene changed again. This time, Ira, dressed in a black robe, was sitting by a stone wheel and near him was a roaring fire in a pit. Ira worked hard shaping a metal object into a hook. In the corner of the small shed leaned a tall wooden stick. He stood up, walked to the fire and thrust his blade into it. After he withdrew it, he was pleased with the curve on it. He placed it in the sand on the side of the fire pit, smiling. The next day, he mounted the curve object. Sarah recognized the scythe. She didn't like the evil smile and expression that danced across his face.

The scene changed once more, Marshall stood with an Anansi, looking in a reflection stone. He lifted his blond bangs up to show his new engraving. "I'm not Murdoc, Bassion. I don't understand why I have this? What does it mean?"

The Anansi grew a bit to reach the tall young man, "You are part Murdoc. It's of a tree with you falling from it. It means you will fail at your new path, Marshall. I don't understand what you are planning, but it won't work out the way you want it to."

"I can't fail. And if my Mother sees I have this engraving, she'll be angry. I have to scratch it off or hide it."

"Doesn't Ira have one?" Bassion sounded concerned.

"No, he doesn't. But he wears that black robe all the time and always has the hood up. He won't show his face to Mother or anyone. I'm frightened of what he's planning."

"We all are, Marshall. You must talk to him. Tell him what you know. What have you learned?"

"I've learned you all are not evil, not like Mother says. And Tomás is right. But I can't say that."

"Why not?" Bassion's voice rose in pitch.

Marshall dug his toes into the soft dirt, took a deep breath and let it out slowly. "I have twenty followers now. They're helping me build a new village away from your village. We're creating our own path in which we don't name Albagoth and don't pair off with an Anansi. We also are trying to find out how to stop the engravings from appearing at age 15. We want to convert others to our way. Some of my followers are insisting you all are evil."

"Evil? We're not evil! Marshall, you have studied under the Sage. You've listened to his teachings and passed all the tests for the Murdoc way. You even have your favorite tree you meditate under. I know it speaks to you," Bassion's eyebrows went up.

Sarah had no idea that spiders had eyebrows or that they could be so expressive or that they could care so much.

Marshall's face turned red. He lowered his face, leaning his head to one side, letting out another deep breath slowly. Sarah could see he felt like he was in a corner. "I do love that tree. Yes, it speaks to me. You're not evil, Bassion. None of you Anansis are evil and the Murdoc people are also very loving. But we need something so different. My Mother would tan my hide if she knew I've been training with you all these years."

"What does the tree say, Marshall? And how will you set up your new path?"

"It tells me to beware of the evil one that will be creating the Black Hole."

"There's no evil one," Bassion started. But a figure in a black robe with his hood up carrying a scythe came up to him, lowered the scythe at the Anansi's neck, and sneered.

"There is now, insect. If you don't fear me, I will destroy all you Anansis and your masters, too!"

Bassion laughed. "Hi, Ira." He expected Ira to put down his hood and smile at the joke. "We have no masters.

We are partners with our Murdoc who shares our life's work."

"I'm not Ira, insect!"

"If you aren't Ira, then who are you?" The Anansi's body shook, though he wouldn't say he wasn't frightened.

"I'm the Wraith!"

"The Wraith?" Bassion relaxed. "The Sage has spoken of the Wraith from world of humans. He brings death and destruction. He's a symbol of rebuilding and rebirth. I have no reason to fear you."

The Wraith pulled the scythe away and swung it again with force, "I will give you a reason!" He enunciated each word as he swung it at the unsuspecting creature, separating his head from his body.

Marshall, wide-eyed and mouth open, "What are thinking? Bassion was my friend!"

"Choose your friends, better, brother. I am reborn. I will bring destruction to all Anansis and Murdocs for rejecting our Mother," Ira replied.

"You know better, Ira! You know the Anansis aren't pets nor are the Murdocs their masters."

"What do you care? You've become a Murdoc sympathizer! Mother has taught you better."

"No, Tomás has taught us better. He taught us to love all beings, including the Murdocs and the Anansis. Bassion was my friend!"

"Anansi can't be our friends, Marshall. They're soulless and partner with our enemies. I've come to wreak havoc on the Murdocs! Those that don't join my Wraith Path will find themselves caught in the circle of my new weapon!"

"No, they won't! I will save them!" Marshall's eyes turned to stone with flashes of fire as he set his jaw.

"How will you save them? You're just someone who is part Murdoc and part god, like me. You will be powerless against my hoard of demons," Ira turned around to leave.

"I will teach love, compassion, and let them know the way of the true spirit is through knowing the Nameless One will adopt them as his children. I will convert them to my way and encourage the Murdocs to follow me to avoid the Wraith and his demons."

The scene changed. Sarah wondered how Albagoth would react to these two. She knew, from her brief meeting with the genderless creator, that nothing escapes its knowing and it always finds a way to correct misconceptions, like these two brothers. The scene came back, drawing her in.

Marshall stood with some of his followers standing around him, outside the Murdoc village. "We teach love and will show them the saving grace of our way of life. We will tell them they don't have to pray to the trees and rocks. Our father above will guide us without using them as a crutch. They are falling short of the wisdom. If they do not, they will be sent to the Black Hole where the Wraith will prepare a special fire pit just for them."

The scene changed, showing Ira practicing his magic, digging a deep hole near a tree that Marshall used to meditate with. His mom came up to him, "Stop this foolishness, Ira. You're play acting the demon has gone too far. I've seen the destruction of some of the village dwellings. My people are your people. I've heard you've even threatened your grandparents."

"I'm not play acting! Mother, your parents rejected you the day Marshall and I were born. I did indeed threaten them and blame them for casting you out, making you give up your crown."

"No, son, they didn't cast me out. I left on my own, choosing to abdicate to the throne when I leave the village."

"I don't believe you. I also blame the nameless god for not claiming us as his children!"

Miriam could see steam coming out of his ears and nostrils.

"Son, I told you and your brother a story that I clung to out of childish wishful thinking. Your father isn't Albagoth, Ira. Tomás, the Sage, is your father. And he has taken care of you and Marshall and did his best to influence you. He just couldn't admit to being your father because of his calling to assist other travelers. Yet, you lost. Come back to see the Truth."

"Truth? I know the truth! You told us to find our own path, Mother. And I did. My path is destroying all who stand in my way!"

"No one stands in your way, Ira. You are standing in your own way. Go see your brother. Talk with him. He knows the truth that I speak of."

"No! Never! He speaks of love and peace!"

"Go to your brother, Ira. I fear he's in trouble and that his followers will turn on him," his mother pleaded.

The scene changed abruptly, showing Marshall with his forehead against his tree, on the other side of it. The hole had been finished, but covered up with Murdoc magic, that Ira denied he had. Marshall's followers came to him, noticing an Anansi was hiding in the tree.

"What you are doing, teacher?" one of the followers asked.

Another asked, "You said not to pray to trees, but here you are, praying to a tree."

"I'm meditating with the tree, not praying to it," Marshall replied. "There is a difference." His new Anansi partner, who shared his engraving, sat above him, silently giving him guidance and support.

A third turned to the others, "Our teacher doesn't follow his own teachings. Look up there, there's an evil Anansi likely influencing his prayers. Come, let's tell he others our teacher is a false teacher who isn't trying to convert the

Murdocs at all! He's a Murdoc sympathizer! He loves them!"

Marshall turned to them, "Brothers and sisters, I tell you, you can meditate with a tree as long as you do not put it before our Nameless father in the sky. Come, heed my words. We can love the Murdocs, but not be one of them."

The scene changed, showing a large group gathering around, carrying Marshall, crying for his death. Ira was in the background, in his black robe and carrying his scythe. He lowered his hood, showing a panicked expression. He rushed through them, chanting a spell to make him invisible.

He grabbed Marshall by the arm, "Brother, trust me. I have a plan and you will be safe."

"Ira, no, you will only get their wrath," Marshall replied. "This is willed by our Nameless father. His will must be done. He will redeem me."

"I am the Wraith, Marshall. I am the one that will save you or drag you into the Black Hole. That will be your redemption."

"That makes no sense," Marshall whispered.

The crowd, half carrying Marshall and half pushing him, chanted, "Tie him to the tree he worships by. Those who pray to trees, die by the trees."

They lifted him up and the Anansis who choose to follow Marshall shot out heavy silk threads which turned to hemp ropes. They turned him up upside down. Ira jumped into the Black Hole, removed the invisibility spell, pulled up his hood and waited for the ropes to be securely tied to his brother. After it was done, the crowd waited. And waited. The sun began to set and the crowd slowly filtered out, not knowing what they were waiting for. Some expected a voice to ring out, because that is the story they all heard from the Sage of Stillness. The voice was to claim their savior as his son whom he loved very much.

Their mother came through, crying and trying to pull Marshall off the tree, but he stopped her. "Mother, this is my choice. I forged my path and wasn't true to it. I was divided in two paths. I cannot adhere to two different ways. This is my punishment."

"No, turn back. I will go back to my parents and take back my crown, train up in the way I was to be."

"Mother, a princess will be born 200 hundred years from now to your ancestors. She will go to the father's world to be raised because her life will be in danger. She will be known as the Lost Murdoc princess, returning at 15, and be the one to merge the three divided paths Ira and I created. Mother, I shall live again."

Miriam, who had been struggling to hold back her tears, began to sob, "It won't work, Marshall. You two divided our world. Now this world is cursed and none of the paths will ever be straight to each village again!"

Marshall, his arms and legs aching from being stretched, and growing groggy from all the blood rushing to his head, struggled to listen. "Mother, your tears have become acid and will fall once a month reminding us of the pain and heartache you have suffered because I have failed you and my followers."

Gradually the hemp threads turned back to silk and slowly frayed. Ira burst up. Those who were still there gasped, "The Wraith is real! He's coming out of the Black Hole!"

The Wraith caught Marshall as the threads completely broke and pulled him in while Miriam tried to pull her oldest son over to her side.

The vision stopped. Sarah stood as if in shell shock. Xander knitted his brow. She noticed there was a man in a red robe with his hood up, wearing a chain with a small circle inside a larger one with many divisions in it. Beside him stood a Snowshoe Lynx. Xander and the man stopped talking.

"Are you alright?" Xander looked at her. "I tried to talk with you, Sarah."

She blinked a few times, replaying all that she saw, but not sure how to explain it. She looked up again, zeroing in on the man with his pet. She noticed his skin appeared to be a light shade of brown and his eyes were almost black, but could be green; they were so dark, she couldn't tell.

"I can't explain it, Xander," she muttered. "Who are you?" she pointed at the man.

"I'm the Sage of Stillness. This is Manx. I'm a traveler, a spiritual teacher who Albagoth called to go from world to world to learn from other spiritual masters and guide others in their own spiritual search. Manx is my helper now."

"You know the twins," Sarah began, but stopped. "You're Tomás. But how is it you're still alive?"

"Tomás? My, I haven't heard that name in a long time. The twins? You mean the legend of the Failed Savior and the Wraith? Of course, I know it. It's a legend here on Wayla," the Sage inserted a finger inside his hood to scratch his ear. "Do you want to hear it? I was explaining to Xander here. . ." He stopped. Realizing Sarah knew more than he was comfortable with. He took a deep breath. "Okay, Princess Sarah, you are in danger and Albagoth sent me to guide you, Xander, Milo, and Geoffrey to safety, but you need to trust me."

"Princess? I'm no princess," Sarah narrowed her eyes.

"Whatever you say. I guess you will have to discover who you are for yourself."

Xander glanced from Sarah to the Sage, not sure what to say or do.

"I'm hungry. Once we eat, we can find Milo and Geoffrey."

"I agree with that." Sarah turned back to the path, her chest tight and her mind replaying key scenes she saw in the vision. She wanted to put as much distance between the

Sage and Xander as she could so she could think, wishing she could visit with Albagoth face to face.

"This place is a maze, Sarah. The Wraiths and the Fallen Savior followers will be looking for you. You have to stay with me."

Chapter 2

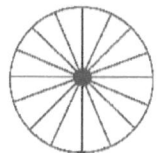

"She arrived," a hooded figure said to another figure dressed in a white robe sitting across on a tree stump.

"Yes, I know. I saw her fall. She was supposed to be alone. Who's the other Indigo teen with her?"

"How am I to know? I don't have the connection you have with the unnamed one," the hooded figure's voice sounded sharp as a knife.

"Maybe he's a bonus to the plan." The figure in the white robe stood up and walked over to gaze down. "I see the Sage is with them. That human doesn't know when to stop talking. Telling too much information, but not giving solid answers."

"Can't we stop him from helping her?" the hooded figure looked up.

"Not sure just yet." He walked away, scratching his chin. "Look, Ira, we must look out for our followers. They need to know the truth."

"Truth? What truth? According to who? May the truth rot in the Black Hole!"

"Watch your tongue! I'm still older than you and you will listen to me," the figure in white said sternly.

"Like black hole I will! You're only two minutes older than me. I came out holding your heel. I was aiming for your neck, but my arms weren't long enough to reach it."

The figure in white clicked his tongue on the roof of his mouth. "If Mom could hear you, Ira.

Wraith wagged his head, mimicking his brother, "If Mother could hear you, Ira." In his normal voice he said, "If Mother could hear us, she'd be siding with you. At the time of your hanging, she even told a lie, saying she lied to us. Neither of us believe her then, right? Or was I the only one who decried her confession as false?"

The Fallen Savior smiled in such a way that the Wraith wasn't sure if it was really a smile or if it was frown trying to disguise itself as a smile. *Harrumphed, only my brother can give a half-arse smile like that.*

"What's wrong, Ira?" Marshall asked, inserting his hands in the sleeves of his robe.

"You. You and your false pity!" Ira picked up his scythe, stood and took three long steps to stand in front of his brother. "I've had it with your pity and 'poor Ira. He's such a failure. He tries so hard to be like me, and he just can't be good enough.' Have you ever considered I don't want to be like you? You're a goody-two shoes! You think you know it all and you don't! You don't even know the name of that extra kid down there with the Lost Princess. Besides that, I've seen another kid and strange animal that is called a griffin down by Shashamé's ocean. Do you know what will happen when Shashamé begins calling that kid and griffin?"

Marshall gave another ambiguous smile, "Yeah, she'll give him some riddle to solve that will help him find his inner connection with All that Is." He wiggled his eyebrows. Ira let out a low growl. Marshall, otherwise known as the Fallen Savior, turned around, folded his hands together, closed his eyes and a bright white light radiated from him.

"No, she will lure him to believe the Nameless One loves him and directs him in all matters. That's such a lie! And you know it!" Wraith fumed.

"Do I really know it?" Marshall asked. "Or do you want me to know it, too?"

33

Wraith growled.

"Where are you off to?" Ira, otherwise known as the Wraith, demanded.

"To listen to the prayers of my faithful followers and direct their dreams." He walked on, then another thought came to him, he turned, "Ira, stay away from your followers and the Lost Princess. Leave it to me to arrange the capture."

Ira let out a low growl again. "Why do you always have to turn on your glow when you leave the room?" he called out.

"Because I can, and you can't. All you do is spread darkness, brother."

"Got that right!" Ira turned back to the clear viewing window. He watched the Sage lead Xander and Sarah to a clearing and gather some rabbits who agreed to freely give their lives so they can eat. Manx and Xander gathered berries and eatable plants, too, to bring to their eating place.

"Like the Black Hole I will stay away! I must do something. Time to re-arrange the trees, shrubs and landscape." Ira marched in the opposite directions of his brother.

As he left, he clapped his hands together leaving the room in total darkness.

Chapter 3

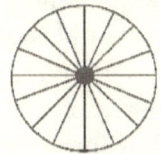

Sarah glanced in the distance, noticing the landscape was moving. She shook her head. Xander and Sage were discussing something, but her thoughts were elsewhere.

A tree bounced up and down, disappearing and then popping up on the other side of the path. Sarah rubbed her eyes. When she looked again, there was a bird standing in front of her, moving its head from side to side.

A bush jumped up and down, and then moved sideways. Xander sniffed the air.

"I smell saltwater. Does anyone else smell it?" Xander asked.

Sarah shook her head, rubbed her eyes and opened them. *I must be seeing things.*

"What's wrong, Sarah?" Sage asked. "You look like you have a headache. I thought eating something and having some fresh water would help.

"It does. It's just I keep seeing weird things," she replied, rubbing her temples.

"Like what?" Sage pulled off another rabbit leg.

"Like a tree jumping up and then disappearing only to reappear somewhere else. I think it's the sun or heat stroke."

Sage and Manx let out a chuckle.

"What?" Sarah and Xander asked with puzzled expressions.

"This place is a maze. When it strikes the trees and shrubs to move, they move. This is how the twins built the world once they finished their main life. They wanted to confuse and mix up all the inhabitants and travelers through here. If anyone got too close to the village they intended to visit, the bushes and trees would move. It is a short cut to getting where one wants to go, but no one can stop the maze. Occasionally the maze acts on its own, as if it has its own life. Be very careful of forks in the road. No one knows where the actual forks come from, but never pick one up. If you do, it will take you some where no one can get to on purpose. A mysterious creature lives there. Its call is the saltwater. Be very wary of the siren's call," Sage explained.

"Fork in the road. You mean when the path splits off in two directions?" Xander asked, petting Manx. The lynx half-closed his eyes and began purring.

"No, it is a fork like the kind you would eat with back home," Sage said.

Sarah laughed, "Yeah, right. That's an old joke. My grandparents used to tell me those old jokes from the '40's, or '50's or something like that."

"It's no joke," Sage assured them.

No one heard Sage mention the call of the siren.

Geoffrey entered the wormhole, and flew on, not seeing where Xander and Sarah landed. He figured they ended up in some other world. Gradually, his wings began to feel heavy and it took a lot to flap them. He yawned. His eyes closed voluntarily.

Milo scanned the land below, thinking they could see where their lost friends landed. He noticed Geoffrey stopped flapping his wings and heard soft snoring sounds.

"Geoffrey, wake up!"

The white griffin's eyes flew open, "What? What did I miss?"

"Nothing yet," Milo said. "We better land. Down there, I think I see a meadow or beach. Not sure from this height. It's getting late and we both could use some sleep. We can find Xander and Sarah in the morning."

"Sleep sounds good," Geoffrey agreed. He scanned the ground with his eagle eyes and saw a spot to land. He dived toward it, spreading out his back legs and moving his tail like a rudder. As they neared the ground he said, "Hold on, Milo. I have to rear back to extend my back legs for landing."

Milo held on tight to the griffin's mane.

Geoffrey reared up as if he was going to stand straight up on his hind legs while in the air, then continued up as if he was going to roll over on his back while stroking his wings. This slowed him down as he extended his back legs and talons, prepared to grip the land. As his hind feet hit the ground, he lowered his front legs and ran until he slowed down enough to stop. Once stopped, Geoffrey looked around the area. It was dusk, so what he saw looked like sand or light-colored dirt mixed with small pebbles and smelled of salty water.

"Where are we?" he asked. "What's that smell?" Geoff asked, winkling up his beak.

"It's saltwater. We're near an ocean or river," Milo answered. "Come on, there has to be a cave or something we can sleep in overnight."

"Ocean? Curá doesn't have those. We just have bodies of water," Geoffrey mused, as he followed Milo.

The day kept getting darker and colder. A slight breeze blew, making it colder. Geoffrey wrapped his wings around himself. They rounded a corner and found a cave a under cliff. They went in. Milo held on to Geoffrey's front right leg and wished for some wood to make a fire and matches. Also some food and vegetables. After eating their fill,

Geoffrey yawned and stretched out. Milo stretched out near him, using his belly as a pillow. Geoff laid a wing over the teen to keep him warm. They fell asleep.

Sound of waves and sea birds calling woke Milo early. He thought he heard someone calling his name while he slept, but wasn't sure. He stretched and yawned, and then scratched himself in different places. Realizing he was thirsty, he wandered out of the cave, not wanting to wake Geoffrey up.

Milo went searching for more twigs and shellfish or whatever he could find.

"Milo, come to Shashamé. Shashamé for Milo. Come to the water. Shashamé will renew you, give you plenty of fresh water and food for you and your griffin friend. Come, dear, weary, Indigo Traveler. Come to me."

Milo paused, listening to the voice from his dream. He remembered that voice. He shook his head trying to dispel it. The voice started over. He realized it wasn't the dream. This woman calling him was real. He headed to the ocean. At first, all he saw was the waves crashing up and drifting back.

"I don't see you," Milo called. Milo squinted his eyes to see better and put a hand over his eyebrows to shield out the early rays of the sun.

A large wave rose out of the middle of the ocean, growing larger and larger, gradually materializing into a woman with long, clear blue hair and a body of a perfect woman wearing a formed bathing top. Her blue-green eyes sparkled like aquamarine stones finely polished. All his senses woke up, he grinned like a small boy on Christmas morning eyeing more presents than he ever expected. He never felt such an excitement when eyeing a female.

"Who are you?" he smiled.

"Shashamé. Goddess of the Sea." She lifted a hand and beckoned, "Come to me, Milo. The water is safe as long as I'm here."

As if in a trance, Milo began walking toward her.

"What do you want with me?"

"To give you your heart's desire," she said.

"You'll help me find my parents?" Milo asked.

"Is that what you want?" the goddess asked.

Milo paused, not knowing what to say. He scanned the sky for the answer, hoping it would be written in the flimsy, lazy clouds that drifted by.

"You do not know what you want. You're a teen with a gift for granting people's wishes, but you have a hard time asking for yourself. You're a writer, dear Milo. A great writer. Use your need to write, to journal to the center of your heart. Asking Albagoth to direct your inner search for what you want," Shashamé reached out a hand.

"I don't have a journal or pen. There are no stores on this world to buy a journal or pen. And if there were, I have no money."

"Money is no object when you can wish you had all you need."

Milo smiled, "Yes, I can do that. But isn't it selfish to ask for myself?"

"No, my son. You have asked for the ability to catch up with your peers in school and be a better student. Asking for a journal and pen is no different." Shashamé smiled, the water particles dripping from her wet hair sparkled in the early morning sun. Milo was mesmerized by her smile and silky, smooth voice.

Back in the cave, Geoffrey woke right after Milo left. He grew concerned for his friend's whereabouts, so he went looking for him. He called his name. When Milo didn't answer, he grew more concerned. He found the teen in the middle of a large, roaring sea. Geoffrey grew more alarmed, because he could tell the teen was listening to something the griffin could not see, oblivious to his surroundings.

Milo stood in the water, listening to the water goddess, "We need food and fresh water. Saltwater isn't good for us to drink."

Shashamé nodded. She disappeared under the water and came up with a container. "Fill this with all the water you two want. When you get it back to your cave, the water will be free of the salt. For food," she yanked up a large net, "Pull this out with you. As you do, it will fill with all the seaweed, fish and shellfish you and your griffin friend can eat. When you two have had your fill, throw the others back in the sea."

"Thank you, Shashamé," Milo stated. He turned to leave, then thought of Sarah and Xander. "Will we find the friends we lost?"

"As the maze and forks turns and confuses those, your friends will be reunited. Be careful of the followers of the Wraith and Fallen Saviors. They are no friends of the Lost Princess. You must find her before the Wraiths do." With that, Shashamé vanished under the sea.

Milo turned around and began walking out of the water. The net wasn't too heavy at first, and neither was the pot. By the time he reached the beach, his head cleared of the trance. Geoffrey ran to meet him.

"What were you doing in the middle of the ocean? You could've been swept away and lost forever underneath that current!"

"I could have? Really?" Milo asked. "I was talking to a water goddess. I can't remember what she said, but look what she gave me." He held up the net which was full of fish, eatable seaweed and shellfish. He lifted the pot, "And this pot is filled with clean water that we can drink. Help me with the net and I'll carry the pot so we don't spill the water."

Geoffrey took the net in his beak and dragged it behind them as they walked back to the cave.

Milo started a fire and strung the fish on a stick and cooked as many as he could. They both ate their fill, which included the seaweed that was captured in the net. Milo found large leaves he formed into a cup for him and a bowl for Geoffrey and then dipped the water out to drink. They had enough for later. They didn't know how long they would be on the beach. But they were full enough now, they just wanted to take nap. Milo only closed his eyes for about fifteen minutes when the water goddess' words came back to him.

While the griffin slept, Milo walked out to explore the other parts of the beach. He found a large boulder and climbed up it. He perched up high, held his hands together and wished for journal, visualizing one with a leather case and strap with a lock. He wished for a black pen and backpack to carry his new journal and pen in, too. In no time, he felt the journal land in his lap with the pen attached to the top. The silver and gold backpack lay at his side. Not sure what to say, he directed his thoughts to *Albagoth, Well, I don't know who that water goddess is, for sure. But she's right. I am a writer. And I don't know really what I want. Do I really want to find my parents and be with them? Or do I want to continue living with the Vey's? Please direct me.*

Milo opened the journal and began writing, asking to be directed to someone who could help him find his inner strength and knowing. As he re-read what he wrote, he wondered where those words came from. He never would have worded his desire quite like that. But it felt right, so he didn't scribble it out.

Next, he wrote, *I don't know where we are. Geoffrey and I were separated from Sarah and Xander. Please help us find them. Please help Geoffrey and I get our bearings and find out what world we are on. We also need to be home within the week because school will be starting soon. I've missed so many cheerleading practices, the captain will be upset with me.*

Geoffrey yawned, stretched, and glanced around the cave. He noticed Milo was over in a corner with a backpack he didn't have before. He rolled his eyes, but figured the teen wished for it for some reason. He knew Xander had his clothes with him in his backpack.

"Now what do we want to do, Milo?"

"We need to explore this beach and find the way to mainland. There has to be place that connects to where Xander and Sarah landed." Milo stood up and stretched.

"How do you know they aren't here?" Geoff asked.

Milo shrugged. "Not sure. I just figured that we would've found them already if they were here. Follow me. I have an idea."

Milo lead Geoffrey back to the sea and began calling Shashamé to come up and speak to them. The water splashed up and down. Out in the distance, they watched as the sea waves increased in size. Milo visualized the image he saw earlier, hoping the waves would form the woman or sea goddess, but instead, a sea creature that resembled a dolphin, but had two horns on either side of his head, jumped up, glanced at them and then opened its mouth and emitted what sounded like a high pitch noise.

"It's laughing at us, Milo," Geoffrey said. "Who are you calling anyway?"

"I'm calling Shashamé. She's the water goddess I was talking to earlier. She's the one that bestowed all the fish and crabs for us to eat. Along with the seaweed," Milo said.

Geoffrey shook his head, "I didn't see anyone standing in front of you, Milo. This world plays tricks on you. Whoever you thought you saw, it was an illusion. Come on, let's start walking in the other direction. I think Sarah and Xander landed somewhere else. Maybe they're on another part of this world and we just need to find a way to get to their side. Maybe if we call to Albagoth, we will see a sign that will lead us to them." The griffin turned away and started walking.

"Where are you going?" Milo demanded.

"Back to the cave to remember how to talk to Albagoth."

Milo sighed as he turned around he spotted a large boulder. He walked over to it, climbed up and sat down. Putting his chin in his hands, he thought about his vision. Maybe Shashamé wasn't real. But maybe she was real. He heard more splashing and heard more of those sea animals playing and calling in their odd laughing noise. He wished he could hear them. At once he heard the words.

"Don't lose hope, Digger. You have been called once. Now you need to dig deep into your being to find that connection. What do you really want in life?"

Milo looked up to see one of the sea creatures looking at him. Another spoke.

"No one calls Shashamé on demand. She comes to those who most need direction. Appearing once, she disappears until needed again. Your friends will come to you. One at a time. Instead, walk the maze and stay with the albino half cat half bird. You two will fight off the Wraith who threatens the peaceful way. Protect the lost Princess until she wakens to her own true self and one true path. She must heal this world."

"Why does this world need healing?" Milo asked the creatures which turned away. Yet he heard one say to his mind, *you will find out, Digger. Remember to write and keep digging for the truth of who you are and what happened during your missing years. And which parents are really the ones who care for you.*

Milo stared dumbfounded at the waves, watching them come crashing in, splashing him, and roll back out. The last words of those mysterious creatures echoed in his mind. Slowly, he walked back to the cave to tell Geoffrey what he

43

learned. Rather, what he did not learn. They gathered their things and began walking to the far end of the beach only to meet with a larger mountain. Geoffrey lowered himself, "Climb on my back. We'll fly to the top and see where this takes us."

Chapter 4

Sarah walked beside Xander and they followed the Sage's footsteps. She wondered what was up ahead and the layout of this world.

"You have to be careful and stick near Manx and me," the Sage called back to them. "We don't know when a path will open up for us to go through it or when it will abruptly close behind one of us."

"Do the twins always control the maze?' Sarah asked.

"No, not always. Sometimes the maze works on its own. It depends on a lot of things. No one has really figured it out."

"Where are we headed?" Xander asked.

Sarah noticed he was scanning the landscape. She wondered if he was looking for something in particular.

"We're heading for the Murdoc village," Sage said.

Sarah quickened her pace to catch up to the Sage. "Murdocs? Why them?" Sarah asked once she was beside him.

The Sage looked at her and flashed a knowing smile, "Because they will have all kind of answers for you, Sarah. And you will have more questions than they will know what to do with. We all know who you are. But you need to awaken who you are. Are you ready?"

"Ready for what?" Sarah asked. Then she remembered the statue of the mother of the twins. "She called me Princess. She said it. But I don't know what she's talking about," Sarah muttered under her breath.

"Who called you that?" Manx asked.

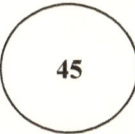

"The mother of the twins. That statue. It sounds crazy, I know." Sarah's heart dropped a beat and she felt an "aha" dawn on her. "No, I can't be."

"You're protected, Sarah. Albagoth will send your Anansi to fight beside you. You have many others who will guide along your new path. It's your choice, Princess Sarah," Sage replied.

"No, no, I can't be the lost princess. I just can't be. I'm just a teen from a small town in Idaho. Nothing special ever happens to me."

"How old are you, Sarah?" Sage looked her in the eyes. She felt a stab of recognition. She didn't know why.

"I'm fifteen. So is Xander and Milo," she added. "What does that have to do with anything?"

"Fifteen years ago the former king and queen gave up their first and only daughter to protect her from the Wraiths and the Fallen Savior followers. They knew she would be endangered if she stayed. And they knew she would return after her 15th birthday. Albagoth would see to it that she returned. It's no accident that you're here, Sarah."

"Don't worry, Sarah, I will protect you," Xander said.

"What if I don't want you to protect me, Xander? All these years, I've been the one to protect you from Butch and his mindless goonies. You are getting better at defending yourself, but I can still knock you across the room when you wake me up."

Xander's face darkened.

"What's the danger in this world?" Sarah asked. "I haven't seen anyone else except you and Manx and a few harmless animals and birds. Where's the danger?" Sarah barked. At that moment, the ground opened and a hand reached up and pulled Sarah under before Sage or Xander could move.

Wraith walked along the dirt road into the nearest village. He stopped at the statue of himself guarding the entrance, dressed in his finest black robes with one hand beckoning all who entered not to rest easy because their torture was just beginning. The Wraith grinned, then quickly put up a gloved hand and wiped it off. He remembered no smiling was allowed in this village. He bowed down at the image of himself, "I am the best there ever was and ever shall be. After all, no one in this world is me. I'm the true Wraith. A master at sending people to the Black Hole." He walked on.

Spying others approaching, he remembered he better disguise himself. He ducked behind a barn and took off his robe. Underneath he wore common cotton trousers that ended at the knee and a V-neck cotton shirt with leather strings and a collar. He rolled up his robe and jammed it inside a wooden barrel. A horse stuck its head out of a window and nibbled on his stringy yellow hair. Wraith batted the horse away.

Voices down at the village square floated to where Wraith stood, observing himself in a window near the horse barn. He turned his head to hear their words better. He headed that direction.

As he neared, he saw a giant Anansi with an engraving of a weeping tree on its forehead and a little man with strange rounded, yet bulging, ears seated beside it inside a cage. He noticed the town folk, dressed in common clothes, like what the Wraith put on, surrounded it, jeering and mocking them.

"You said the Lost Princess was on this world. You two are supposed to be the sooth-sayers of your Murdoc village. Tell us where she is so we can string her up," one of the women sneered.

"I said no such thing. What I said as it is prophesied she would come, but no one has seen any strangers here. We have news of strangers by Shashamé's beach. But no one ever ventures over to her beach. We all know she's a siren and could lure others to their doom," the Murdoc man said. The Anansi elbowed him in the ribs with one of her legs.

As Wraith got closer, he saw the little man had an engraving of the same weeping tree. He knew the symbol meant they revered the trees and communed with them freely. But these two were not the prophets of the village. They captured the wrong Anansi and wrong Murdoc man.

"Release these two. These are not the two you need to find the Lost Princess. I know where she is! She's with the Sage who taught your mighty Wraith demon and his demonic brother, the Fallen Savior."

"Marshall is not the demon. Wraith is the demon," the Murdoc man answered. "How do you know we aren't the right two these people wanted?"

"Yeah, how do you know? You're a stranger to this place," another asked.

The Wraith villagers all turned and glared at Wraith.

Wraith glanced down at himself. He realized he was wearing tan and black. He wanted his black clothes. He muttered something, waved his hand over his clothes and turned them black.

"I'm the mighty Wraith," he said. "I've come to lead you all to the Lost Murdoc Princess. She is here to disrupt our way of life. We cannot afford to live peacefully with these Murdocs while they worship the one who shall not be named."

"You mean Albagoth?" said the Anansi.

"Yeah, that's what he means, Jacca," said the little man. "We don't worship Albagoth. We just respect and honor the genderless one for creating this world and all worlds. This is what the trees have shown us and indeed what all who come here say."

"Again, how do you know these two are not who we want?" Another asked.

"I know because of their engravings. The prophets of the Murdocs have engravings of ankhs or a star, moon and sun intertwined. These two have weeping trees. The weeping trees symbolize teachers. These two teach others to commune with the trees and nature," Wraith explained.

"How do we know you're the Wraith? You aren't wearing a black robe and don't have your scythe. Our mighty Wraith has better things to do than come up here to lead us to find the Lost Murdoc Princess." The others cheered him, echoing his words.

"How do you know this?" Wraith asked. "What makes you an expert in knowing me?"

The one who spoke last walked up to him, taking off his hat with one hand and pulling out a necklace of the Wraith with a hand out, beckoning others to come. "The real Wraith gave this to me when I was but a child. He told me I would become leader of the coven here on Wayla. He told me to pave the way for others to follow the dark course, scaring Murdocs and enticing others to kill, maim and burn down all they loved. I lived by Wraith's words. I have followed his words and teachings to the letter. If you were truly him, you would know all of us by name. It is written in our dark book of curses to dishonor all who are beholding to the Fallen Savior and kill all Murdocs." His follower jutted out his chin.

Wraith gulped. He paused, his mind spinning. He remembered that little boy and he knew his encouragement of him would end up bad. But he did it anyway. He searched his mind for the name of this man standing opposite him, challenging him.

"You all are Murdocs, too," called the little man in the cage.

"No, we are not! How dare you say that!" screamed the crowd. Others stuck sticks inside the cage and poked him and the Anansi. Others threw stones, which the Anansi batted away with a touch of his legs, turning the stones into annoying insects.

"Hee, hee, that tickles," Jacca giggled when a stick poked his side.

"No, it doesn't tickle, it hurts! And annoys me!" The little man yanked the stick out of the man's hand and turned into a snake. The snake looked in his eyes and listened mind to mind Once the snake understood, it nodded its head and slithered away down his leg and out the cage. The adults closest to the cage ran away screaming. The others just laughed.

"Such tricks and tom-foolery," Wraith called to the Murdoc. "What do you call yourself, little man?"

"I'm Petra. You're right, Jacca and I aren't the prophets. We're the teachers. Two of the many teachers in our village. If you are indeed Wraith, then you will also answer to Ira. And you know you have Murdoc blood flowing through your veins just like these people. We know who you are. We aren't afraid of you."

"You should be," The Wraith said to Petra.

"No black hole is too dark for us," Jacca added. He smiled, waved a left leg and shrugged, adding, "Besides we all know you couldn't have dug the black hole without your Murdoc magic."

The interrogation was interrupted abruptly with a scream. The Wraith didn't know what the person yelled, but it sounded like "Help!"

"We caught something! Come look!" someone yelled from way down the road, followed by someone running down the gravel path towards them.

Some of the attention to the Murdoc and Anansi turned towards the new villager approaching.

"Look, Joahnna says he caught something. Let's go see what he has!"

"What do you mean he caught something?" Wraith inquired, looking at the leader.

"We have a trap door near the desert where the glass rain comes down every two moons. Something must have fell through it. Joahnna and others take turns watching to see if someone will fall through. Usually it is an animal or straying plant life creature. Something else must have come down this time."

All those surrounding the caged Murdoc and his Anansi, including the leader of the group, fled to find out what they just captured, leaving the Wraith with the prisoners. He narrowed his eyes. Petra smiled.

"Ira, we go back a long way. I've lived many moons and remember when you and Marshall were young. Before you two began the stuff of legend and deities here. I remember you two having both human and Murdoc blood flowing through your veins."

"Lie! Mamma told us that the nameless one is our father and he denied us. If the nameless one is indeed our father, then he should come down here and claim us!" Ira shouted.

Petra softened his face, yet withdrew them inward as he searched deep within himself for what this angry and hurt Wraith needed to hear. It came to him.

"I wish to help you with your anger. I'd be angry, too, if my father didn't claim or accept me. Albagoth is creator of this world and many more. That doesn't make Albagoth your father in a physical sense. Albagoth is a genderless spirit who speaks to us through the breeze, and in meditation. We offered to teach you and Marshall how to commune with the trees and with Albagoth, but you wouldn't listen to us. Marshall did. He hid this from you. There's many things your twin hid from you. So much, I don't even know it all."

"You lie, Petra! I do remember when we were young and learning to meditate with you all. I renounce it. All my inner voice told me was to reject your words and listen to it. It spoke of how delusional you Murdocs are. If I had both human and Murdoc blood, then why hasn't my human father came forward?" Ira shook a fist at him.

"Maybe because he wasn't able to. Who has spent the most time with you and Marshall? Think, Ira. Think back to that time." Petra spoke softly.

Ira thought back, remembering the Sage coming to visit and how the Sage used to greet his mom with a hug and often lifted her off the ground and swung her around. The Sage always took them out to the beach and spent time with the sea sirens and other sea creatures. The Sage also spoke of Albagoth, but not as their father, but as a guide. And he taught them to meditate, too.

"Peace comes to you through quieting your mind and slowing down your heartbeat. In the gentleness, the one true voice will speak to you, showing you the way you need to be," the Sage always said.

"Baaah, the Sage was a goody-two-shoes! When we really needed him, he was never there. He never told us where he'd disappear to or how he came and left from our world," Ira growled.

More raised shouts and whoops came from far away. Sounds of a stampede came towards them, interrupting their conversation.

"We will have another chat, Petra. I'm not through with you."

"We look forward to it, Ira. Many blessings. Remember the path leads to within. That is where you will meet the true Albagoth," Petra smiled.

The villagers came back leading a blond-haired teen dressed in Trip pants, army boots and black tunic towards them.

"We caught us another Murdoc. She doesn't have an engraving and says she isn't from Wayla. She says she's from some world called Nampa in another galaxy. Whatever that is," the leader of the village told the Wraith.

Ira smiled. They caught the Lost Princess. Ira watched as the young teen squirmed and protested.

"Let me go! Who are you and why have you put me in chains?" Sarah yelled.

"Shut up, you freak! Why don't you have an engraving?" the one holding her chains shouted back.

"Maybe it's because I don't know what one is. Maybe it's because I don't belong on this world. We came here by mistake!" Sarah tried to pull away.

Someone behind her punched her in the kidneys. Sarah kicked backward connecting with his most painful area, hearing him cry out in pain made her smile.

"You're a girl! Where did you learn to fight like that?" the leader said.

"I have brothers! I've had to fight all my life to keep them from beating me up," Sarah said through clenched jaws. "If you see girls as weak, why do you have strong women in your guards?"

Her question was ignored.

"Put her in the cage with Petra and Jacca," Ira commanded. The leader set his jaw, clenching his fist and strode over to Ira, poking him in the chest

"Who made you leader of this village?" said the leader.

"Don't touch me like that!" Ira lifted a finger and flicked the man, causing him to fly across, knocking over the villagers who were standing there, holding Sarah's chains. "I'm the Wraith! I'm the one you all pay homage to and torment all Murdocs and Fallen Saviors in my name. I'm here in person, you will obey me," Ira said.

Petra snickered. As the two squared off.

The leader picked himself up, snarling more, brushed himself off. "I still don't believe you! If you are who you say you are, you would know my name. You don't even recognize me."

The leader's words struck Ira like a blow across the face. Anger rose from his belly. He fumed, as many counter arguments swirled in his mind like whirlpools threatening to pull him under. Inside his mind he heard, *Be calm, Ira. His name is Razbuator. Call him Raz."* Petra winked at him.

Why are you helping me? Ira thought back to the Murdoc teacher.

Because you and I used to be friends a long time ago before you decided you were a god and could be the worse demon this world has ever known.

Ira's expression changed, to stunned silence, his thoughts swept away by a mere memory of them playing so long ago. *That would make you over 200 years old, like me.* The imprisoned Murdoc smiled and nodded.

Now speak to Raz and don't be friendly. He needs to believe you. It would be better to be your scariest demon self, though. He respects hateful and those who can overpower him.

Ira cleared his mind and focused on Razbuator, remembering the day he appeared to the young boy, crying alone in a dark attic, fervently praying to Wraith to assist him to smite his tormentors. Ira remembered bestowing on him the symbol the adult leader now wore.

"Razbuator, I remember you, a weak, vulnerable youth, crying because others called you a lily-livered Murdoc, saying you could never be a true Wraith because you weren't mean or angry enough. I bestowed you that charm, urging you to get in touch with your inner demons and allow them to rise to the surface. You have surpassed all I knew you would. But now, I command you, as the one who made you, to leave that teen girl alone. She's not from our world. We have no real knowledge of what her race or world of origin is. Put her in the cage with the Murdoc teacher and his Anansi," Ira's voice and words rang out deep like a kettle drum.

"We do know she's a Murdoc," said the young boy, who pulled Sarah down the hole. He pulled her filthy blond hair back revealing odd shaped ears, reminding Ira of the dread cauliflower his mom used to feed him and Marshall as boys. "Her ears look just like that Murdoc over there."

"Proves nothing!" Sarah elbowed the kid hard in his stomach, causing him to bend over.

Razbuator stood opposite Ira, humbled a bit, yet still sneering, "Someone told you that memory. Or you stole it from my mind."

"If I stole it from your mind, then doesn't that prove I'm who I say I am?" Ira lifted an eyebrow.

Raz leaned his head to one side and brought it back up, "I suppose so." He paused to reflect. "Okay, boys, put the captive in the cage with the freak teacher and his gross companion."

His followers pushed and pulled Sarah towards the cage as Sarah stiffened her legs to prevent them from dragging her. Instead, the tallest and most muscular of the women punched her in the stomach and then put her over her shoulder and carried her to the cage.

Raz stalked over to Ira, eyes narrowed and jaw set, glaring at him. He spoke through clenched jaws, "I still don't believe you are the mighty, fearful Wraith. If you were, you would allow us to torture this young female and get out all her Murdoc secrets out before we put her to death. We know the Lost Princess is supposed to be coming back soon. It's up to us to prevent her from taking the throne. Are you with us in killing all Murdocs and protecting our way of life? Or do we need to condemn you to the Black Hole, too, the way you condemned your brother?"

Wraith smiled. The skies darkened and thunder rang out and the bolt of lightning struck a nearby tree. When the sun came back, Wraith stood there in his black robe and scythe in hand, "You do know who I am, Razbuator. If you didn't, you wouldn't have said I condemned my brother to the Black Hole. I am who I say that I am. I am the only Wraith that ever walked Wayla."

Raz's mouth fell open. The Wraith turned around and left the way he came in, knowing he had the upper hand now.

Chapter 5

The Wraith villagers grabbed Sarah by the elbows roughly pulling and pushing her toward the cage. She dug her toes into the soft dirt mixed with stones with all her might, doing what she could to prevent them from treating her like a villain. A massive sized woman, built like football linebacker approached her and punched her in the stomach, hard. Once she was bent over, she hefted Sarah up and over her shoulder. Sarah cried out and then pounded the woman on her back with her bound fists.

I hate feeling like a helpless wrench, Sarah thought. *Albagoth, not sure you can hear me. I know you hear Xander. But am I just as important as him? If so, please help me to get out of this place!*

"Stop beating my back, your wretched Murdoc! We have no use for you people. Especially for ones that refuse to admit what you really are!" the woman's voice boomed.

"I know what I am! I'm human!" Sarah protested.

Others around roared with deep belly laughs. One of the men opened the cage door and the woman carrying Sarah threw her inside. She landed on her belly, knees, and side of her face.

"Oww! That'll leave a mark!" she cried out, but tried to say it soft.

Those that heard laughed harder.

"Stay on your belly. I'll tell you when to move," came a soft reassuring voice near her.

Sarah waited, listening as footsteps retreated away from them. Laying there, she imagined a spider in front of

her with a symbol of a circle with many divisions on it. *Don't worry, Princess. You're in safe hands. Petra and Jacca will take good care of you. Listen to their guidance. And go within to find your strength in Albagoth,* it said. Sarah wasn't sure what to think, the words were comforting in a way but also a bit disconcerting.

"Who are you?" Sarah whispered back, trying to look up at her cage mates.

"I'm Petra and this is Jacca, my Anansi mate."

The last of the footsteps faded down the gravel dirt road. "Do I dare move now?" Sarah asked.

"Yes, it's safe now, your highness," Petra said.

Sarah looked up to see the little man bowing to her and the spider was also bowing to her. She screamed.

"There's a spider near you! Kill it!"

"Spider? Where?" Jacca swiveled his head and eight eyes every which way.

"It talks! What are you? And why are you two bowing to me?" Sarah wiggled like a worm, doing her best to sit up with her hands still bound. Once she sat up, she stared at her two cage mates.

"You're the Lost Murdoc Princess, your highness. We've been expecting you," Petra sat up.

"I can't be. Though, that statue of that woman and those two deities said I was. I just can't be. I wasn't raised here . . ." Sarah's voice trailed off. "I've always felt like I was just dropped into Nampa from some alien world," her words came out in a low whisper.

"You were hidden from the Wraiths and the Fallen Saviors for protection. We knew you would be back after your 15th birth year. We've been prepared for it. Unfortunately, so have the Fallen Saviors and the Wraiths, too."

Stunned speechless, Sarah stared at the Murdoc, then moved her eyes down the cage floor. Her mouth opened and she heard her words as if another was speaking for her, "How did you know?"

Petra smiled reassuring her, yet Sarah felt like he was condescending.

"We have contact with Albagoth and the Universal communications."

Sarah lifted a hand up to scratch her forehead, but the other hand came, too. She let out a frustrated grunt.

"Jacca, please go over and unlock the Princess' hands," Petra asked. The Anansi crawled over, Sarah screeched and tried to back away.

"I don't bite, your Majesty. I am tame and trained to teach and be sociable," Jacca comforted. He gently took her bound hands in one of his legs and put another leg over the ropes and muttered some words Sarah couldn't make out. The ropes fell away.

Sarah's mouth fell open, she rubbed her wrists. "Thank you, Mr. Spider."

"Not spider. I'm an Anansi. I'm at your service. I'm also willing to teach you how to access your own Murdoc magic and the voice of Albagoth."

"Okay," Sarah drew out the last two letters. "Go on, please tell me more about who I am . . ."

"You might not understand it since you were raised in a different world. Our King and Queen had to give you up to protect you. When they did, they changed the way our village was governed, temporarily ending the monarchy. The Wraiths and Saviors were destroying us left and right. Once the prophecy came down that the last heir would be lost to another world, we knew we had to hide you. If we didn't, they would have killed you while you were an infant. You will find a way to unite the three paths and restore the monarchy. We know you will," Petra finished.

Sarah played back his words, shaking her head, "No, I can't be the one to fulfill the prophecy. I'm part human, aren't I?"

"No, you aren't," Petra snapped, then abruptly stopped talking as Jacca punched him in the side. Sarah noticed that all eight eyes on the Anansi were narrowed. "I mean, your father will explain that to you as soon as we can get ourselves out of here."

Sarah nodded, wondering how they would be released or get themselves free. She heard footsteps behind her. She turned around to see who was coming. She scooted back to sit between Petra and Jacca to get a better glimpse of who was approaching them. A dark cloaked person with his face down walked in measured steps.

Gradually, the sun began to set.

"It's too early for the sun to go down," muttered Petra.

The cloaked person paused at the cage but didn't lift his hood. Sarah spotted the symbol of the circle with many divisions on a chain around his neck. It sparked a memory, *The Sage had one like it. I need to find out why that symbol keeps popping up for me.*

"Mystery is all around us, Petra. You three are safe. Do not fret or worry. No harm will come to the Princess."

The voice sounded familiar, but odd. Sarah was sure she didn't know it.

"We trust Albagoth, creator of all Worlds," Petra replied.

"Who leads us all to the path that best suits us," the cloaked stranger said.

"And all paths lead everyone within themselves," Jacca replied.

"Albagoth has passed down these words from eons to eons across the galaxies," the hooded figure replied.

"We are already whole. We are our own savior," Petra and Jacca replied.

"So be it, in the name of all Good and all Oneness," the hooded stranger replied.

The cloaked person took his hands out of the large sleeves and circled in front of himself, moved them inward making a smaller circle, and then brought them together and then separating them, then moved each hand opposite each other as he made two paths, and bringing them back to the inner circle. He repeated the movements in different directions until he made six or more different paths that all met at the inner circle, finishing with his hands together in a prayer form and let out a peaceful sigh. Then he vanished.

The three of them sat in silence, soaking in what they just witnessed.

After a while, Sarah spoke, "Who was that? Or did I just imagine someone there speaking odd?"

"It was the Sage of Stillness," Petra said.

"But how? Xander and I were with him when I fell down that trap door." She paused, "Or maybe I was pulled down it."

"It was both, Princess," the Anansi answered.

"The Sage can be in two places at once. That's the gift Albagoth gave him when he was chosen to be a prophet for the Creator of All Worlds. He helps us teach meditation and nature relevance in other worlds. We are the chosen, but that doesn't mean we are special, as such." Petra glanced at her.

That didn't sound right to Sarah. Frowning and shaking her head, she said, "No, you Murdocs aren't the chosen ones. That's supposed to be the Fallen Saviors, right? I mean, their savior was hung from a tree, so they think they're special and that their savior will come again. Right?"

Petra laughed. "No."

"NO?" Sarah spoke the word with a hint of outrage. "No! You will not contradict me! I don't know how I know, but I know Murdocs are not supposed to consider themselves better than the other spiritual paths on this world. We are all equal status and Albagoth has given us the same gifts. It's just that the Wraiths and the Saviors do not accept them. One wants to destroy everyone and the other wants to destroy only the Murdocs because they hate being reminded of who they came from!"

Sarah harrumphed as she crossed her arms in defiance.

Her words slapped both Petra and Jacca. After a few minutes, Petra started smiling and gradually began laughing. Sarah refused to smile or budge. Hearing his jovial laughter angered her even more.

Finally, she asked, "What's so funny?"

"You do remember, Princess Sarah. You have the seed knowledge of all Murdoc lore and the lore of this world deep within you. I was testing you by saying we are the chosen ones. You are who we say you are. And your experience with Raindom in the Shadowlands last week shows this."

"How did you know about that?" she asked, stunned.

"We are connected to other worlds and Raindom now has access to his ancestor's roots now that you opened up the Shadowlands. He is most grateful to you."

Sarah's stomach rumbled. "I'm grateful to him, too. He showed me a piece of myself." Her stomach roared. "Will they feed us?" Sarah asked.

"No, we have to free ourselves and then Jacca and I will lead you to our village. We can eat there. Now, rest for a bit while Jacca and I prepare to free us."

Sarah scooted up to another corner, still a bit grossed out by the spider-looking creature, then laid down, yawning. "Why didn't the Sage free us or stay?"

"What we saw was his spirit essence. He's with your friend, Xander. They're safe, we hope. Sleep now, young Indigo Traveler."

Sarah saw herself strolling through an open pasture, no breeze and a few birds chirping. Only the blades of grass moved slightly. In the distance she heard an eerie call, *Sarah, Lost Princess of the Murdocs. You've come to re-arrange the paths of Wayla. You're still lost to yourself. You don't know who you really are or where you belong.*

You belong to two worlds, the human world you were raised in and the Murdoc world you were born in. No memory of this birth world resides in you. Wake up! Meet yourself. Meet the person you were born to be.

She watched herself staring out in the distance. The golden circle with the many divisions in the middle of the field. It drew her to the middle, "What do you mean?" she asked in the dream.

The answer resonated all around and inside of her, "Go deep within yourself, Sarah Ohman Ahama, Princess of the Murdocs. It will only be revealed from a deep meditative state. Your Anansi will guide you."

A face of an Anansi with the engraving of the symbol of its forehead appeared to her, "Hello again. We will be meeting in face to face in a waking state soon. We are much closer. All of your answers will be coming soon." It paused, lifted a leg closest to his medium sized head and scratched the side of his head, smiling. "Well, maybe not all of your answers will be questioned. I mean, not all your questions will be answered. If they were, then you'd stop growing." It chuckled.

"Right," Sarah replied dryly. "Um." She woke up, feeling no fear of the spider. She didn't understand why her fear wasn't as strong. She sat up, seeing the cage door open and Petra and Jacca were standing outside, waiting for her.

Stars dotted the sky, sparkling Christmas lights back home. Sarah realized she was homesick. *School will be starting. I need to find Xander, Milo and Geoffrey. My parents will be worried sick about me and Xander's parents will be worried, too.* She thought a minute, *No, my parents won't care where I am. But Xander's will be concerned about him and Milo. And Xander said his mom found Milo's parents.*

"Coming?" Petra's words jarred her out of her sleepy thoughts.

"You were going to leave without me?"

"Not a chance, my lady. We allowed ourselves to be captured so we could protect you and lead you safely to our village. The Wraiths are asleep. Ira is likely back in his realm, plotting his next move against us Murdocs."

Sarah rubbed her eyes and yawned, stumbling along behind the little man and his spider looking friend, replaying his words. Her thoughts switched to how they opened the cage.

They walked to a clearing, stopping in a vine bush. The night's orb shone bright. Petra knocked on the vine bush. It sounded like he was knocking on wood.

"How did you unlock the cage?" Sarah asked, ignoring why a vine bush would sound like a wooden door.

"It wasn't locked from inside, my lady. We Murdocs have a way with locks. We needed you to sleep so you wouldn't see what you're not ready to know. Once we get to our village, I will introduce you to your teachers and you will meet your Anansi partner."

"What about my birth father? Do I get to meet him and find out why I was given away?" Sarah asked, stuffing her other concerns about why Wraith is so bent on hurting her people down in the deepest pit of her stomach that she could.

The vine bush opened, showing that it was a door that was covered in vines. They entered a pure black hallway with eerie glowing lights mixed with high pitch hissing, snapping and clicking that reminded her of tarantulas make when annoyed. A different noise came in above the other, sounding more like drumming and a cricket rubbing its legs together. The last sound was much closer to her.

Petra prodded Jacca, "What did they say, Jacca?"

"They said Marshall came down for a walk about. His followers are rounding up, meeting to discuss plans to raid our village in search of the lost Princess. We need to hide her. Marshall visited our village afterward, saying he will do what he can to aid us to protect her. But we have to trust him."

"I won't trust him. Not after what he did to my father back before he was strung up that tree. We need to see Shashamé."

"Not now, Petra. Think, we need to train Princess Sarah."

Sarah shook her head, rubbed her eyes. As she replayed the words, anger welled up deep inside and rushed out of her mouth, "Stop talking about me as if I'm not here!"

A twig snapped, Sarah felt someone grab her arm, "Hush."

Sarah grabbed the hand and forcibly removed it.

Petra whispered, "Sorry, Princess to speak to you like you weren't there. We must be quiet. We aren't the only ones in here. Keep your voice low."

"Hello, this is a Murdoc entry way. Who's there? Show yourself."

"Don't call me princess. I'm Sarah."

Sarah heard a swish sound, like someone struck a match against the side of a box and fizz. The hallway brightened with a flame.

"Calm, peace and soul reassurance to you, Brother Petra. It's me, Marshall. The Anansi announced my coming before I could surprise you."

Sarah narrowed her eyes to examine this new man standing there with a light shining all around him, and realized the light wasn't from a match at all. It centered around the tall, dark haired twin of the Wraith. His features were much darker, more olive toned, and face slender, yet his nose chiseled, like someone chipped away at a stone boulder to create him. He wore a white robe that was wrapped around him like a towel. She wondered where his turban was, surely in this heat, he would need a turban to keep the hot sun from baking his brains. "Oh my god! I didn't just think that, did I?" she gasped under her breath. "How rude of me!"

She closed her eyes, further seeking to see more about who this person was and what secrets he held. Gradually his secrets came revealed themselves to her. She didn't understand how she was getting the information, but he came to her in snapshots, words and moving pictures, like someone was showing her a documentary on his life from boyhood to this present moment.

They all looked at her.

Marshall's light flared, turning more of a reddish orange flame, "What are you talking about?" Marshall, breaking character, demanded. "We're having a serious conversation over here or trying to and you're busy muttering about turbans and towels and other garbage. What's wrong with you?"

Sarah growled, "You're supposed to be the savior of the Fallen saviors and you're so rude yourself. If you knew anything or were truly on the Murdocs' side, you wouldn't be concealing yourself in their hidden passage way that only they are supposed to travel through."

"Good point, Sarah," Jacca cheered.

"I created this entry way before the Murdocs claimed it. My twin, Ira and I created it when we were kids over 200 hundred eons ago. The Murdocs claimed it and used their skilled magic to conceal from my followers and the Wraiths. So don't get so high and mighty with me! Besides, you're new to this world and don't have the proper knowledge to get all comfortable with correcting your elders, young lady!"

"I'm no lady, mister! Please don't mistake me for one! I'm Goth and not afraid to wear black. When I get home, I will get a tattoo and even dye my hair. As far as I'm concerned, you're no savior of this world, either! You're just a misguided fool who has tried to scam these people!"

"Watch your tongue, young Indigo Traveler! Or I will take you over my knee," Marshall threatened. Sarah stalked up to him, fists balled, staring him straight in his hazel eyes.

"I'd like to see you try!"

Marshall hissed, glaring back. For once, his holier than thou attitude had gone out the door. The more he considered Sarah's cold, brown eyes, the more he felt lasers searing through him, cutting out his heart, and continuing down his middle, sawing him in half. He exhaled, relaxed and settled down.

"Where did you get your fire, Sarah?" Marshall asked. His light suddenly dimming.

"I'm not sure. You bother me. I thought your brother was annoying with all his bravo on being the baddest dude to walk this world. But you're worse with 'I'm so holy and you're not . . .'"

Marshall's light went out totally, his mouth fell open.

"Hold it! I don't act like that. I mean, I used to. But not now. Do I, Petra?"

"We go way back. You have changed over the years. Marshall, let's get out of this entryway and we will discuss in around the village fire and nice large bowl of stew."

Chapter 6

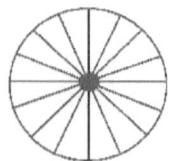

Xander glanced around him, wondering where Sarah disappeared to. The ground just opened and swallowed her. Even though he saw it with his own two eyes, he couldn't believe it. He felt a mix of panic and shock.

"We need to find Sarah," he called up ahead to the Sage.

"Don't worry, Xander. Your friend is safe. She'll be with her birth family soon," Sage called back.

They walked in silence. This world was full of pastel colors, deep blues, trees full of orange and purple leaves, bushes where you can pick orange berries that taste more like a sour cherry than an orange and yellow strawberries that taste like. . . Xander didn't know what. They had a unique taste and texture.

The smell of saltwater came drifting to him, bringing him the found memory of being near the water a few weeks ago before they left for Curá. Xander sighed. "I miss my home," he mused under his breath.

Xander, come to the sea. Play on my beach. Listen to the crashing and thrashing of my waves. Rest your weary bones. What you seek you will only find in my waters.

Who are you? Xander sent back.

Shashamé. I'm Shashamé. Your friends were here on my beach. Come. You will find all you seek.

The words came to him as if through water or a tube, jarring Xander, giving him the sensation he was underwater, drowning. He saw himself thrashing about.

Something jarred him, shaking and pushing, shoving him around.

"Alexander, don't listen to her! Xander come back. You're not underwater. You're on dry land," Sage commanded.

Xander shook himself. "Um," he started, but couldn't find the words or thoughts to finish the sentence. He ran his fingers through his thick, black hair, stiff with a week's old dirt and sweat. *I need a bath.* He ran his fingers over the week's old stubble, realizing he forgot to bring a shaver with him. Suddenly, the skin on his cheeks and chin began to crawl.

"Are you okay?" Manx asked, nudging him from his other side.

"Yep, I think so. Hey, where are you leading us? I mean, me?" Xander absent-mindedly began scratching Manx's head and ears.

"You will know when we get there, Xander. You need to trust me. Remember, don't listen to Shashamé."

"The beach is calling to me, though. Where is it? She said my friends were there."

"We will find the griffin and Milo. Don't worry," the Sage replied, sounding more like a cold commander of an army than a wise Sage and guide.

Not sure I can trust you, when I really don't know where we are or who you really are. Maybe the ground will swallow you up next. He felt a stab in his gut, alerting him he shouldn't have said that. *Albagoth, I'm not sure why I resent the Sage. I don't know him. He's leading us into circles. We need to find Sarah and the others and this guy doesn't care about them or me. What am I supposed to?* The answer came to trust, but he couldn't bring himself to do that.

Manx turned around and came back to join Xander.

"You're concerned about us not being honest with you and that you think we're leading you astray, isn't that right?"

Xander tightened the shoulder straps of his backpack, clenching his jaw, weighing what to say and what not to say. "Yes, in a way. I don't know you and the Sage. You two just dropped into this place, like we did," Xander corrected himself, "I mean, you just materialized here like on those space exploration shows."

Manx laughed. "The Sage loves those shows. And yes, we're capable of materializing wherever we need to be. Except, once on the world we need to be on, we can't just materialize to the next place. But the Sage is capable of being in two places at once."

"Really? How does that work?" Xander sneered. "He said Sarah was okay and was with other Murdocs. How does he know?"

"Because he can divide his spiritual self away from his physical body and go where she was held captive," the Snowshoe Lynx explained.

Xander shook his head, not sure he wanted to believe that.

"That sounds impossible," Xander exclaimed.

Sage turned around, with a piercing look that sent a chill through Xander's being. "We met on Curá a week or less ago. In the Crow Court Realm. I counseled you to be careful in the Shadowlands. You don't recognize me, do you?"

"No, because that person I met looked much older than you are now," Xander replied, a bit more heated than he planned on it. "And it was dark, too, if I remember right."

"You're the one that lives in darkness, Alexander. You rely on Albagoth to be your savior instead of taking responsibility for yourself. Before you met Albagoth, you relied on Sarah to fight your battles. Now suddenly, you want to be her savior. Don't you realize her Murdoc magic makes her stronger and more able to see through another than you will ever be? You're jealous she was able to open the Shadowlands for the Crow Judges to come in. She stole your thunder and you aren't just jealous, you resent her."

"Resent her? How can I resent her when she's the most beautiful gal I've seen? Girls are supposed to be weaker than us boys. Someone has to be her protector."

As Xander listened, he noticed with amazement the trees and shrubs moving as on a platform, forming a wall behind the Sage, who was walking backward. The Sage didn't notice the silent movement of the landscape.

"No, Xander. Sarah being full-blooded Murdoc will always be your protector. And that griffin of yours is also your protector," Sage admonished.

The Sage took measured steps behind himself, as if he knew where to place each foot as he chewed Xander out, came to sudden halt backed into the wall of thorny bushes and trees. Another set of trees and ground covering opened a path to the left; the colors sparkled and popped, drawing Xander's attention away from the path. He turned down it, without thinking.

"No, Xander, don't go that way!" Sage and Manx called together. Xander couldn't hear them, though. They watched helpless as their charge wandered off without them.

"Now what do we do?" Manx asked, slowly wagging his sagging snub of a tail.

"I'm not sure," Sage muttered. "I suppose we use our own power inner strength to discern what to do."

"Perhaps we go to the Murdoc village to talk with Davineh and the Wisdom trees," Manx suggested. The Sage nodded in agreement.

Saltwater filled the air and a light breeze carried small droplets of water, splattering Xander on the face, refreshing him from the heat and sweat. The sun was now at his back. The path gradually inclined, causing Xander to lean forward and he found he had to change his foot placements. His heart rate and breathing increased from exertion. He paused to catch his breath, scanning the hill.

Xander couldn't see the hill at first, so it surprised him. Something inside him hoped this would lead him to where Sarah was. His mind flashed a memory from his gym class, the teacher showing the class how to recover quickly from running or climbing by bending over. He bent over. As he did so, he felt dizzy and thirsty. He wondered why he was in this world and still didn't know the name for it. *Albagoth, did you create this world, too? Can you hear me?* Those words hit an invisible wall and bounced back to him. He sighed. *I suppose I'm on my own with no guidance from you this time.*

Xander sighed as he began walking again. The sun began to go down. As he neared the top, he heard voices coming up over the other side. The hairs on the back of his neck rose to attention and all his senses became sharper, too, as he scanned the field for a place to hide in case there was a threat. Two shadows, long and narrow spread out towards Xander, increasing the desire to run. One of the shadows looked like it had knives on either shoulder and long flappy ears and the other was shorter, but thinner and could be carrying something deadly. Xander reached for his own sword, remembering it was in his backpack. He lowered it and began fumbling with the zipper. The voices grew closer and he realized he knew them.

"Hello?" Xander called.

"Xander?" Milo answered.

"Yes. Milo? Geoffrey?" Xander called. Before they could answer, Geoffrey took flight, picking Milo up in his talons and flying down the hill. He dropped Milo right in front of him and they embraced. Geoffrey landed and embraced both.

"I'm so happy to see you!" the three said together.

"Where were you?" Milo asked. "I mean, where did you land?"

"Not sure. We landed in some field where strange glass-like particles were falling from the sky. It burned my skin, when it hit. Sarah had this magic bracelet that she claimed Jephra gave her," he scoffed, "that she turned into a parachute, which also covered our bodies protecting us from the space and solar storm as well as entry into the planet's atmosphere."

Milo nodded but zeroed in on only one part of what Xander said. He noticed that Geoffrey also narrowed his eyes at what he said.

"You doubt Jephra gave Sarah that bracelet?" Milo asked.

"Well, yeah. She's a girl, why would Healer Jephra give Sarah that bracelet when I am more deserving? After all, I'm supposed to be the Indigo Traveler," Xander thumped his chest.

Geoffrey laughed. Xander's mouth dropped.

"You're supposed to be my friend and protector, Geoffrey. What's the laugh for?"

"Do you know what my Grandsire said to me after you left Curá that first time, Xander?" the griffin asked.

"No, what did he say?"

"He said you weren't the only Indigo Traveler in your world. He knew there would be more coming. He also said Milo was an Indigo. Often you Indigos can't recognize each other and when you do, you believe you are the only special ones out there. It's isn't true. I am your friend, Xander. I will always tell you the truth and stand up for you. But I will also tell when you are deluding yourself. Like now."

"How am I deluding myself, Geoff?"

"By thinking Sarah isn't deserving of that bracelet. In fact, I remember Healer Jephra calling her over to the side, and taking her into his tent, saying he had something for her. It's obvious to me that he saw something in her that said she could wield that power and use it properly."

"So, could I!" Xander huffed.

"That isn't the issue, Xander," Milo replied. "You're jealous, and hurt that Sarah stole your thunder. Get over it. We're in a strange world and we could be in danger. Where is Sarah?" Milo glanced around. "She's supposed to be with you."

"The ground opened up and swallowed her," Xander said. The others laughed. "I'm serious, guys. This world is totally alive. The trees and shrubs move on their own and the ground opened like a trap door and something pulled Sarah down. The Sage said something about a Wraith dude that moves everything around on a whim," Xander said, raising one shoulder and waving a hand as if to push away the words.

"You don't believe it?" Geoffrey responded.

"Not sure. It's folklore on this world. There's this statue of a Wraith guy pulling another man down this hole and a woman crying, trying to pull up the falling fellow. Anyway, I lost that Sage dude back on another path. I got to find Sarah."

Milo looked at Geoffrey, who nodded and they both looked at Xander. "No, we three will find her. She could be in danger," Milo stated firmly.

"What's the big deal? Sarah's a big girl. She can take care of herself!" Xander glared at Milo and then Geoffrey. With hands on his backpack straps, he began marching up the hill.

"Where are you going, Xander?" Milo yelled.

"Up this hill, in case you can't see."

"What's your problem?" Geoffrey yelled.

Xander didn't answer.

"We've been that way, we need to go back here, I think," Milo yelled.

"All will be lost if we lose him again," Geoffrey stated softly to Milo. "I'll go get him." He glanced at Milo to see him nod in agreement. He began flapping his wings, ran a little bit and then jumped in the air. He grabbed Xander by the shoulders just as he reached the top of the hill, and then turned around.

"Ouch! Your talons are piercing my skin, you stupid griffin! Let me go!" Xander wiggled.

"No, I won't. We found you after being separated for almost two days. We aren't going to let you out of our sight. You're going to stick with us so we can tell you what Milo found out."

"Fine!"

Once they reached Milo, Geoffrey put Xander down and the three of them sat there. Xander told them about the Sage of Stillness and the statue and Milo told him about what the water goddess said.

They paused in silence for a bit, each thinking what the other said.

"Do you really think Sarah is in trouble?" Xander asked.

"Not sure," Milo answered. "Shashamé, the water goddess, seemed to think she is. You mentioned that the Sage of Stillness mentioned the myth of the lost Murdoc princess. I think he may know more than what he says."

"I didn't see this water goddess," Geoffrey scoffed. "So I don't put much belief in what it told Milo. I just know we need to find Sarah. I'm entrusted with keeping the three of you safe and out of harm's way. If anything happened to any one of you, your parents will not forgive me."

"Sarah's parents don't even know where she is. That's another reason we need to find her and get back home soon as possible," Milo added. "I probably missed my cheerleading practice, too, and that will get me in trouble with the coach."

The three went silent again. Thoughts tumbled through their minds. Geoffrey's stomach rumbled, like an angry monster.

"Hey, do you trust this Sage of Stillness? Maybe we can find him and find out what he knows," Milo suggested.

Geoffrey's mind flashed to the night of his Grandsire's funeral prier. He remembered a cloaked figure coming to sit with him. Intuitively, he knew who he was. It was the Sage of Stillness, warning him to go after Xander in the Shadowlands. Maybe, just maybe, this was the same person.

"I know we can trust him," Geoffrey stood up, stretching out his front legs and body, and then walking his front legs back as he extended his back legs and then hunched up his back, like a cat. He yawned.

"How do you know for sure?" Xander asked. "He appeared creepy, in a way. I felt like he's hiding something. Not telling me the full truth."

He studied his two friend's faces, glancing back and forth. Both wore puzzled expressions. "I can't put my finger on it. He knows more about this world than we do."

"He can't reveal everything to us. We should explore on our own. But if this world is as dangerous as Shashamé told Milo, then we better stick together," Geoffrey stated, standing up and stretching.

"And watch out for moving trees, bushes and shifting ground," Xander added. The three friends moved off to the left, not sure where they were going.

"Let's find some food," Geoffrey suggested. His stomach roaring again.

"I could use a double cheeseburger, onion rings and a large chocolate milkshake," Xander ordered.

"I'd take a large veggie wrap with a side of French fries and large Lemonade," Milo followed suit.

"Those sound awful. I wish for a herd of any large mammal that has juicy meat on its bones. I'll even eat it cooked," Geoff added.

They giggled, as all three of their stomachs began to rumble.

Chapter 7

Sage looked at Manx, shrugging.

"Now what do we do?" Manx asked, wagging his snubby tail back and forth slowly.

The Sage lifted his left arm, shaking down the sleeve of his black robe, revealing a bracelet with many buttons and settings. He began punching some buttons. "We go to the Murdoc village to make sure Sarah is safe. Then we go into invisible mode to observe the Fallen Saviors and their planning."

"What about your wayward sons?" Manx asked, standing up on his hind legs, putting a paw on the Sage's right shoulder.

"Don't call them that, Manx. No one is to know. In fact, they don't even know who their real father is."

"No one is around us now, Sage."

"True that, but still. These woods and paths have ears. Ready?"

"Ready."

Sage pushed the final button and they vanished. They reappeared in the outskirts of a village. It took them a while to re-orient themselves after the transportation. Manx blinked his eyes and shook his head. Sage put a hand up and rubbed his eyes and then used both hands to massage his temples.

"We really need to go to a technology advanced world next to get that device serviced. It's beginning to give me headaches," Sage sighed.

"Me, too," Manx agreed. "But I can't rub my temples like you can. Wish I could turn my front paws into hands."

Sage leaned down and rubbed his temples for him. "Is that better?"

Manx purred in response, kneading the ground and rubbing against the Sage's leg. Twigs snapping and the ground rumbled telling them they weren't alone. Sage straightened up and Manx perked his ears.

"Who's there?" Sage called.

"It's just me, Sage."

"Who's 'me'?"

"It's me, Gertrude, Terrence's Anansi. Davineh sent me to fetch you." A large Anansi came out, her eight eyes sparkled in the sunlight that filtered through the trees and bushes. On her forehead was an engraving of a cross with a loop on top. It signified her office as one of the leaders of the eternal life ministry.

Sage bowed from his waist to greet her, "All is well I take it. And the Lost Princess has been found?"

"Yes, she is with us. But we are not safe. Marshall is here. He begs an audience with you. Davineh is doing his best to prevent it. Petra and other prophets are saying there will be more attacks. Especially after the Fallen Savior Village know for sure Princess Sarah has returned. Right now, though, we have more pressing issues. Princess Sarah is resisting what we tell her and she isn't happy with Davineh for giving her up. She doesn't understand. What do you suggest? After all, it was you who took her to the World of Nampa and placed her with the human family unit of Johnson."

Sage inserted his hands within his large sleeves as he studied the ground.

"Did you hear me?" Gertrude repeated.

"Of course, he heard you, you Ninny. He's thinking!" Manx snapped.

"Sorry!" the Anansi hissed through clenched jaws. "You do remember, cat, that I spit venom at my enemies, right?"

"And I can squash you as if you were a tiny ant!" Manx hissed.

"Stop! Neither of you are acting like mature, spiritually in tuned animals. Remember, we're on the same side," Sage broke up the spitting fight.

"First, Gertrude, take me to Davineh. Remember, Marshall is the deity of this world so he can have an audience with anyone he deems important enough."

"Not going to happen. Marshall is suffering from a big case of self-doubt since Princess Sarah chopped him down a little bit. She doesn't know the sharpness of her tongue and she also isn't in touch with her inner Albagoth voice," Gertrude explained.

"So, introduce her to her Anansi and begin training her to meditate and how to commune with the trees. When she gets back home, she will need those abilities to guide the next Indigo teen that comes to her. He is on the wrong path and needs her guidance to find the right one."

Gertrude shrugged. "Whatever, Sage. You're the one we go to because Albagoth talks directly to you and you are able to see the Creator of All Worlds face to face whenever you need to."

"My dear, Gertrude, you can, too. As a teacher of meditation and wisdom, that is open to you. All you do is go within with the intent to see Albagoth's face."

Gertrude sighed, rolling all eight of her eyes, knowing he was right. "Yes, I know. I've done it many times but trying to teach this Princess how to do it is difficult. She has no desire to see Albagoth's face. Said she saw the Creator of All Worlds a few days ago and has no desire or interest in why she needs to continue to seek the genderless being every day."

The Sage clicked his tongue. "War is coming, Gertrude. We need to protect her and get her to understand the danger we all are in if she doesn't tap into her inner knowledge to figure out how to unite these three paths to either prevent the war or end it peacefully."

"You're scaring me, Sage."

Sage sighed. Manx attempted to suppress a giggle, until the Sage gave him the evil eye. The three walked into the village in silence.

Sage's mind filled with memories of the twin boys' youth, watching them the day they were born and seeing them walk. He remembered sitting with them on the beaches of Shashamé's ocean, regaling them with stories of the Creator of All Worlds, explaining how all the different worlds were made and why each was so different than the last one.

"But we on Wayla are the special, too, right?" Ira and Marshall both exclaimed.

Sage remembered squirming in his seat each time they brought this up.

"Mama says we are the children of the Creator. The creator fathered us, right?" Marshall asked.

"But he won't claim us. So should we acknowledge him?" Ira followed up.

Sage remembered his oath to the boys' mom never to tell them the truth. She loved the stories about the Creator that fathered an actual son or daughter and wanted her boys to believe those ancient human legends. She believed it made them special and want to become much more than ordinary Murdoc boys. Though, she and Sage knew the boys were half human. So much could change.

This line of thinking brought him to what to tell Sarah. He had to find a way to open her mind and spiritual being to embrace her people's mystical knowledge. A glittering light off to the left brought Sage out of his musings.

"When did Marshall get here?" he asked Gertrude.

"I mentioned he was here, Sage. Sarah tore into him, so his light has dulled. In fact, he's afraid of go near her and others. I think he's sulking."

"Ain't that human of him," Manx joked.

"Don't tell him that," Sage and Gertrude both hissed.

"We have ourselves quite the situation. We have a lost Murdoc Princess that believes she's human and a Fallen Savior that is half human but doesn't know it and yet refuses to acknowledge his Murdoc self," Sage muttered in an aha moment. *Please, Albagoth, guide me how to get through to each of them. Somehow, I failed to own up to the truth to the twins when they were little. I allowed Miriam to have her way.*

"Lead on, Gertrude. I'll think of something as we enter the village," the Sage sighed solemnly as he inserted his hands in his long sleeves, hoping the right words and actions came to him.

Sarah sat by a small pond staring at the water. Out of the corner of her eye she noticed a small sapling moving toward her on shaky roots. She ignored it until it toppled over into her lap. She glanced at it, helping it up.

"Are you okay?" she asked it.

"Excuse me, your highness," it said in a toddler voice. "I didn't topple over. My parents told me to come bow before the returned princess."

"Bow? To me? I'm no one, young tree. I'm just a teen from the World of Nampa. Please don't bow before me," Sarah replied.

"You aren't just any one, your Highness. I've been sent to urge you to travel within yourself."

"How do I do that?" Sarah was intrigued, yet annoyed. She wanted to be alone with her own thoughts now that Xander and Milo weren't with her.

"I've heard whispers you feel lost and alone. You were taken as a young sapling away from Wayla and given to a world that is not your birth world. The parents who accepted you were not aware of how different you are even though you appear so very human," the young sapling continued.

Sarah thought of her own confusion about noticing the differences in the others in Nampa and herself. She had visions of divisions, and weird glimpses of fractions within herself. Her mother couldn't explain the strange interests Sarah had with wanting to touch trees. Sometimes she felt like she could just melt into one. As a young toddler, she used to play with spiders, but then one bit her. Now she's terribly afraid of them. She always wondered if her parents truly loved her. How can anyone truly love her if her original parents gave her up? Not only did they abandon her, they took her to a whole different world. Surely, she did not sign up for that when she decided to be born into a body.

"How do you know so much for such a young tree?" Sarah asked.

"It's part of my training. It's the knowledge that all Wisdom trees are sprouted with that goes way back to our ancestors from the eons and eons when Albagoth planted the first one."

Sarah touched the young tree's leaf, considering what kind of a tree it was. "You're a Banyan tree, right?"

"In some worlds we are called Banyan trees. There will come a young Indigo boy that will need your guidance and protection, Princess Sarah. You must journey to find your fractions and unite yourself. Before you can heal Wayla of the divisions, you must unite yourself and find Albagoth deep within your heart and soul."

Sarah's eyes narrowed. The words felt hallow to her. "How do you know I'm divided? I don't even know what that means. Hey, do you have a name?"

"I'm called Little One. I haven't been officially named yet since we Wisdom Trees are named after we're 24 months along and begin to shape our character. I'm barely 10 months. Some of the elders say I have the wisdom of a 110-month-old."

"How long do you live, Little One?" Sarah sat up, wishing to know more about it instead of her journey.

"We live for eons. After a Wisdom tree is well over the 900 months, we begin saying they've lived for eons."

"You can transport me to anywhere I want to go?" Sarah asked, smiling.

"Yes and no. Some places only the Murdoc healers and your assigned Anansi will take you."

The Scuttering of eight feet snapping twigs and shattering and crunching dried leaves interrupted their conversation. They turned to see an Anansi standing there.

"Sorry, Little One. Pardon me, Princess Sarah, I'm Nickoli. I've been assigned to you. Your birth father wants to speak with you. We understand your frustration and anger, but the only way to work through this is to listen to us and allow us to guide and teach you. There is much for you to learn. We also have news that the Wraiths and the Fallen Saviors may be organizing to invade us. We have to prepare."

"I don't see how they can when we have Marshall in our village. I think he's hiding out from his followers," Sarah said, standing and brushing the dirt from her black pants. "I'll come with you, Nickoli. I'm ready to listen to what my birth father has to say. Maybe even to take the journey that Little One was telling me about."

Sarah sent her thoughts to Albagoth, not expecting a response or how the genderless deity would respond. *Xander always talks with you, but I've never heard him say how you answer him. Do you use signs? Or some other means? I mean, really, I don't know why we're here. I'd say we came by accident, that Geoffrey got blown off course, but now it looks like we were blown off course for a reason.* She sighed. *I need to know what I'm supposed to do.*

A little voice deep within her replied, *Listen.*

Listen to who?

Listen to Nickoli. Listen to Davineh. Listen to the trees and to the Sage. Mostly, listen deep within yourself. Express yourself in ways you have never expressed yourself before. Visualize yourself. What do you really want? Where is it you want to be? See unity and listen to the Wraiths, and the Fallen Saviors and see beyond the physical bodies of all before you.

Sarah sighed. She wasn't sure if what she heard was Albagoth or part of herself guiding her. It confused her, in a way. Though, the words made sense and awakened a desire to know more.

As she followed Nickoli and Little One, Sarah reflected on the missing pieces that the little tree mentioned to her. She understood. Often, she felt fractured, like there were parts of missing. She knew for a long time she wasn't truly a Johnson by birth, but her parents didn't treat her any different. Her older brother did, though. Or teased her about it. Her mind wandered to Xander. She hadn't thought of him since they got separated. It felt like two days since they last saw each other. She hoped he was okay. She knew he fought King Titus two years ago, and she wondered then how he managed to do that without her there. She saw him as a weakling. Really, what can he do to protect her? That's laugh, him wanting to protect her, when she has fought all his battles with Butch since the seventh grade. Now they will be freshman at Columbia and she hoped the bullying would ease up.

In some ways, it had, because Xander came back different, a bit more self-assured, but his mind was still in the clouds and he still refused to work hard to get his grades up. And then there's Milo. Sweet, tiny Milo who is built like a football kicker who enjoys doing gymnastics, hiding the fact he can move mountains just by wishing and knowing he can do it. Milo enjoys being popular, but clearly doesn't fit in with the guys at school. He loves hanging with the cheerleaders. Yet his best friend will always be Xander since they were in pre-school. Their friendship goes beyond that in that they are more like actual brothers than friends.

She sighed again, looking around her. She could've sworn the trees and shrubs were moving again. The ground rumbled. Surely this place didn't experience earthquakes or Wayla quakes, did it? Then she remembered how the ground opened and swallowed her the other day, landing her in a cage in the Wraith Village. Her eyes widened as her breathing came in short bursts, and her heart began to race. Glancing around, she realized Nickoli and Little One were way ahead of her.

"Hey, guys, hold up!" Sarah yelled. "The ground is shaking and . . ."

Just then, the landscape opened like a doorway, and a figure dressed in a brown robe with the hood up came out and grabbed her, putting one hand over her mouth and the other around her waist. Sarah struggled, kicking her left foot back, connecting with his groin. She thrust her arms up between his hands and yanked them away from her mouth. Once the figure removed its hand and bent over in pain, she turned and stomped on its other foot. Then turned to run, only to be caught again by two more figures in brown robes with their hoods up, hiding their faces. One of them lifted her up and threw her over the shoulders of the taller figure. Sarah kicked him in the chest and pounded her fists on its back.

Chapter 8

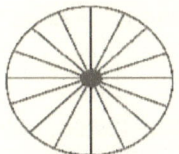

"Won't do you any good to pound on my chest and back, missy. We got you and we ain't giving you back to those goody-two-shoe Murdocs. Quit your protesting," came a voice that was both a deep male tone and gentle feminine.

"If you don't leave the Uni one alone, we will knock you out, princess!" came another voice, much deeper than the first. The way that person said princess wasn't respectful at all. A fire deep in Sarah's gut ignited and rose to the surface.

Her mind went blank as visions of a being clothed in brilliant white and indigo colors, standing in front of her lead her in a prayer, moving his arms in a circle as he spoke, "This represents all the worlds that Albagoth created. These are the many paths," he began to move each hand down in sections, "that lead to the inner circle that is Albagoth. Albagoth leads us to within ourselves." When he was done, the being removed his hood and dimmed the light. He looked into Sarah's inner eye and spoke, "You, Princess Sarah of Murdoc, are commissioned to unite the Wraiths, Fallen Saviors and your Murdoc people. They do not have to accept the Murdoc way, but realize their path is one of many that Albagoth approves of. They need to say his name with respect and not fear the Creator of All Worlds."

How do I do this? I'm not even sure who you are or who these people are that have kidnapped me.

"I am the Sage of Stillness. You haven't seen me in my spirit form. Trust yourself. You will be trained further when you get free. Right now, go within on your own. Albagoth left a part of itself inside you. Genetically your Murdoc magic has been passed on to you. Just allow your mind to go blank and trust in the essence of the Creator of all Worlds to guide you. Also, call on the Wisdom Trees to speak to you through their root system."

The vision vanished. Freezing air and cold stone jarred Sarah. She opened her eyes, wrapping her arms around herself to see she was laying on the floor of a cell. She heard footsteps approaching. She wondered how long she was out. Soon a tall, slender, narrow faced man stood in front of her. He stopped at the cell door to look at her. He wore a tree in full bloom around his neck.

"Greetings. I understand you're supposed to be the lost princess of the Murdoc clan. You don't look very threatening."

"I'm just a teen from the World of Nampa," Sarah replied. "I don't consider myself very threatening. Not sure why you and the Wraiths want to hurt me."

The fellow laughed. "You don't understand the prophesy surrounding you, do you? If you take the throne, you will destroy us. You will wipe us out or make us become full Murdocs. We will never ever join that hateful bunch. They worship trees and speak of the nameless one," the man spit out, frowning.

Sarah smiled, "You say they worship trees, yet you wear one around your neck. How can you be so afraid them, yet idolize them?"

"We Fallen Saviors don't idolize the trees. They are the symbol that caused our Fallen Savior to die."

"Tell me how he fell?" Sarah asked, realizing if she learned more about them, she might be able to see how to help them.

"He was weak. He preached love of all, and to tell all about the good news that we don't have to go to the trees for wisdom. The wisdom is around us, and we were to persuade the Murdocs their way was fool hardy. The more our leader, before he fell, spent time with the Murdocs, listening to their elders teach, the more he became convinced their way wasn't evil. He switched his teachings to include their way, except he refused to say the name of the nameless Creator, as he taught us."

"Why was that?" Sarah grabbed the bars, showing intense interest, while her mind worked on how to convince him to let her out.

"According to the legends handed down, the Nameless Creator was his father who would not claim him nor his twin brother," the man said.

"His twin? Isn't the twin called the Wraith?" Sarah said. "His real name is Ira, right?"

"I don't know. Maybe. We just know he's the evil one that entices everyone do wrong. You know, entices the kids to disobey their moms and dads. Entices the women to be strong and not rely on their husbands and tells girls they are as good as the boys and can be anything they want to be."

"But girls can be strong and do anything the boys can do. On my world, we know we are better than the boys," Sarah's eyes twinkled, as her mind replayed memories of her arguing with teachers and babysitters about what was proper for a young lady to do. She usually won. Always the stubborn one, refused to go along with the stereotyped girls must be mommies or play with dolls. She was always the rough and tumble one, ready to wrestle any boy that tried to accuse her of being a soft, weak 'girl.' "I am a girl, what's it to you? Just because I'm a girl, doesn't mean I can't whip your bottom on those rings over there or out run you!"

"In the Murdoc Village, the women and men equally do the chores and share the leadership," Sarah said.

The man shuddered. "We aren't Murdocs and we won't ever become like them. We have to keep you from ascending to the throne because you will force us to become like them!"

Sarah laughed. "You fear me? Why? I'm just a teenager. I don't have any powers. You all are Murdocs, though. Like humans are all humans even though some have dark skin, some are light skin and some appear to have yellow skin. It's all based on where the sun is in their ancestors first originated from."

"Really? On your world, there's people with different colored skin?" the man pushed down his hood, his eyes wide, intrigued. "Does it hurt to have different color skin?" His chiseled features bore into Sarah, striking her as someone who is naïve and trusting.

Sarah laughed. "It only hurts if they get a sunburn from being out in the hot summer sun too long. It doesn't matter about the pigment. Other than that, no, it doesn't hurt. Does it hurt to be separated from your village of origin?"

"I don't understand what you mean," the Fallen Savior follower knitted his brow.

"You were deceived by the Fallen Savior and the Wraith. You all are Murdocs." Sarah paused, considering her words, hoping she was getting this right. She was stabbing at straws right now, knowing she hadn't been fully trained in her Murdoc gifts.

"How do you know?" he asked.

Sarah considered him some more, before answering. She wondered how Xander saw into individuals. Right now, she could use his gift of seeing through to the secrets this man held close to his chest. She weighed her options. Telling him the truth verses bluffing her way through it. Then she realized she needed his name. Names are sacred in some places. Were they here? Once you name an object or a person, then you have some control over him or her.

"What's your name?"

"Name?" he was puzzled. "What does my name have to do with our discussion? You're avoiding telling me how you know so much about what our Fallen Savior endured or what he told us or kept from us! Also, he would never join forces with the evil Murdocs or his shifty, good for nothing brother, the Wraith!"

"Names are everything," Sarah beamed. "I'm Sarah Johnson from the World known as Nampa. And you are?"

"There's no other world known as Nampa! This is the only world that matters!"

Sarah started to burst out in laughter, but quickly slapped her hand over her mouth.

"What's so funny?" his voice went from anger to puzzlement. "I'm serious. The creator who created this world has no business creating other worlds when he can't even own up to the boys he fathered. What business does he have creating more unfathered children?"

Sarah shook her head. "I don't know. I'm going on my gut. Look, I must call you something. I'm going name you Thomas."

"Gut? What do you mean you're going on your gut? Guts digest food not think! We think with our heads!" He tossed over her words. "What's a Thomas?"

"Thomas doubted once that the savior in one of my world's creation story came back from the dead. You doubt Albagoth cares about the people on this world. Albagoth is a genderless spirit. He created everyone or made it possible for this world to support life. But your Fallen Savior is not a physical offspring of Albagoth. I've heard he is part Murdoc and part human."

"That's a blatant heresy! How dare you demean our Fallen Savior! Only we can demean him and blame him not ridding Wayla of all the bloody Murdocs!" Thomas roared.

Sarah sighed. She wasn't getting anywhere with this man. The interrogation had gotten totally off track and she didn't know where to take the questioning. It occurred to her that Thomas was supposed to be interrogating her, and not the other way around.

Thomas drew his eyebrows down, shooting invisible arrows at her, his nostrils flaring with each angry exhale.

"What say you to the charge of pre-meditated wiping out all paths that are not Murdoc?" he accused.

"I plead not guilty. First off, I've only been in this world one or two days. I don't know my way around here and have yet to be fully trained in any specialty," Sarah shrugged her shoulders. Her mind flashed on how each of the Murdocs she's seen had tattoos on their foreheads. She lifted up her bangs, "Look, I don't have a tattoo, either. If I were a Murdoc, wouldn't I have a tattoo?"

"Tattoo?" Thomas appeared taken aback by the strange word. "You mean engraving? Well, maybe your engraving is there, but it hasn't revealed itself yet. I've heard that you Murdocs are born with those engravings and they only come reveal itself when you realize your path and place in the world."

Thomas appeared shaken for a minute, pushing back his hair and scratching his neck. He turned around a few times. It was then that Sarah realized this man was just a boy.

"How old are you, Thomas? You're hiding something. Aren't you?"

Thomas hung his head, took a deep breath and exhaled. "Yeah. I'm only 13 eons and this is my first time on my own questioning you or any Murdoc. This isn't going very well." He lifted back his own bangs to reveal an engraving of a paths, a boulder with one path going around it to the left and one going around it to right.

Sarah shook her head, "I don't understand. What does that mean? Your symbol?"

"It means I walk a divided path. I am raised to be anti-Murdoc, but all you say resonates deeply with me. I have dreams of Albagoth and wake knowing Albagoth has been talking with me, guiding me and directing me to help you. Only thing is, if any one of the leaders in my village find out, I will be ex-communicated. How can I help you?" he whispered.

"You can get me out of this prison cell and help me get back to my village so I can complete my training," Sarah replied. "I have one question; did you have someone engrave you?"

"No, it just appeared on my forehead once I began having dreams of Albagoth…as the genderless one began to train me in how to help you."

"Will it change once you choose a path?" Sarah asked.

"No, it won't. Only, I will choose which path is right for me. It might change, I don't know. It's just, I can't risk anyone here finding out I am a marked Fallen Savior."

"I see. Okay, so where do we go from here?"

Thomas glanced around him. They heard yelling and running outside in the streets. Then a door down the way opened and footsteps came towards them. "Look, back away from the cell and pretend I've shaken you up a bit. Act afraid of me and terrified for your life. Once we get out of this, I will find a way to get you out."

Sarah listened to him, scooting back towards the wall, she messed up her hair and found dirt on the floor to rub on her face and clothes.

A taller man came in dressed in beige tunic and baggy black trousers with his hands inside his large sleeves. He glanced at Thomas and then Sarah. He smiled, sending chills up and down Sarah's spine.

Calmly, he withdrew his hands from his sleeves, slowly. His face showed stern concentration as if he needed to think hard on the action. Once they were out, he lifted one of his palms outward, and spoke solemnly, "What are you doing with this prisoner, Darrel?"

"The name is Thomas," he answered. "I'm interrogating her, trying to get information we can use to infiltrate the Murdoc village soon and make sure she doesn't take the throne."

"I don't believe you," the man glanced down at the ground, slowly, with effort, lowering his hand, "Our Fallen Savior has whispered in my ear that there is a traitor among us, Darrel. You've been named that since birth, but now chose to go by a different name. A name she gave you. . . ."

"How do you know I didn't choose that name for myself, Father?" Thomas said. "It's the name the old Sage of Stillness used to call me when he could visit and teach among us."

"How foolish that false sage is," the priest said, dismissing Thomas' explanation. "He's forbidden to enter here because he did his best to warp your young minds to believing the Nameless one has no gender and the Murdocs are harmless. We know that is not true. They are the ones that mislead our Fallen Savior. We must do the work he could not. Now, please step aside."

Sarah stood back, watching and listening to this man and Thomas discuss the pros and cons of their mission versus the Murdocs. She wondered how she was going to free herself, while being bored at how slow this man or priest was speaking. Listening to him was like listening to her science teacher speak about atoms and molecules fighting. She yawned and gradually her eye lids began getting heavy and closed automatically while imagining atoms and molecules circling each other and colliding, creating colorful yet frightening explosions.

All at once, a loud explosion occurred outside of her cell. Sarah's eyes flew open as she saw that doors of her cell were wide open, smoke was everywhere. She coughed and did her best to wave the smoke and debris away. As it cleared, she saw the priest had been thrown through the wall landing out in the road. She stepped out, cautiously, "Thomas, where are you?" she called, looking every which way.

"I'm over here," he called, meekly. She looked to her left, turned around, to find him on the ground against another wall to her right. He was stunned, but okay.

"What happened?" she asked.

"You. You used your Murdoc magic to blow our spiritual leader out of the hallway, thus ending his indictment of me as a traitor. Come, Princess, help me up. We must go. I know how to get you back to your people. But you must tell them to accept me. I can't come back here now that they know I am of two paths."

Sarah extended a hand and he took it, she pulled him as he pushed himself up. Thomas stood up, brushed himself off, looked around for his staff, found it and they took off out the new doorway and down another path. Thomas led her to a new maze, waved his right hand and it opened. They went through it and vanished into the entrance of the Murdoc village.

It was an odd sensation, as Sarah went through the passage way. It was like going through a hallway filled with gelatin. It sucked and popped as if she had just immersed her whole body in a Sarah sized tub filled with slime. The kind of slime she and Xander used to play with as grade-schoolers. All she could hear were voices that sounded like they were underwater. Or maybe they were under water. Her gut told her the horrible truth that Thomas wasn't experiencing the same sensation as she was. *Okay, Albagoth, I'm not sure about this. I should trust you, I guess. I can't see Thomas. I know the passage way he opened leads to my birth village, yet somehow, I'm lost and alone. Show me what to do.*

It is not me you need to trust, Sarah. You need to trust yourself. All you need to survive is to open your inner being to your spiritual essence. Trust yourself to channel your magic that you were born with.

You mean, like that dream of the atoms and molecules exploding together? I didn't plan that. I don't even know what I did to cause it to happen. How can I trust myself? I mean, isn't that a given? Also on my world, those in the mainstream spiritual paths talk about trusting their god. Aren't you like their god?

I am Albagoth, Sarah. I am not a god in the manner of those in the mythos of the world you were raised on. I am the Creator of All Worlds. I urge those who recognize me to go within to see their own power to become their own creators. Each has free will. You need your Anansi. Where is Nickoli?

We got separated when I got captured.

Sarah sighed. She noticed a spark of light, like a star appearing briefly, grab her attention away from her internal conversation. She turned to it to see it better, only for it to disappear. *I know Nickoli can help me. He said he would teach me to center myself and use my abilities. But I am so confused, Albagoth. I really don't know anything about being a Murdoc. I thought I was human, only I don't fit into the human race. I am not even sure I fit in with the Murdoc people, either. And aren't all the people here Murdoc? It's just that the Fallen Saviors and Wraiths appear more half Murdoc and half human or something.* She sighed again. She followed the path where the sparkle appeared and disappeared.

"Sarah, come this way!" Thomas called from a different path. "You're going the opposite way from your village.

His voice sounded different. It sounded more familiar, but she wasn't sure where she heard it before. She saw an image of Lynx, the werecat from Curá. But that couldn't be right. How and why would Lynx be on this world?

Albagoth's voice came back to her, *Thomas isn't who you think he is. The one the priest called by a different name is at his home, asleep. This one is a friend and will lead you to the right path. First you need to call him by the name of the vision you saw. Trust, my daughter. Trust and be rewarded.*

Those words struck her like an odd statement. Basically, she wasn't supposed to question.

"Lynx, come this way. I saw a sparkle of light. I think we need to go this way."

"It's a trap, Sarah," Lynx came to her, still in Thomas' shape. "How did you know it is me?"

"Your voice betrayed you. How did you come to take that shape? I didn't think you could change into a human?"

"I can change how I want to. I just usually prefer to be a lynx. On this world, in the village you were held prisoner, it was safer to be one of the Fallen Saviors who is going to be leaving his family's path to follow the one that is calling to him."

"Thomas is a real person?" Sarah inquired.

"Yes, but that isn't his name. I didn't know his name, so I adopted the one you gave me. The leader of the pack, the one I called Father, is the one that said his real name. I think he called me 'Darrel.' I always could read minds, or get glimpses of what others are thinking. I just seldom use it until Albagoth requested I come here to look after you four. I choose not to read minds, though, unless I need to. Like now."

Lynx glanced around at the path they walked on. "Are you sure this is the right way? It doesn't feel right to me."

"What do you mean it doesn't feel right?"

Lynx shrugged. "I'm a werecat. I have a natural animal instinct to sense energies around an area. This way. . ." he searched his mind and thoughts, "makes my fur stand on end. I sense enemies around us getting ready to spring. We need to get you back to your people."

Sarah paused, wishing she knew more about reading energies and knew how to tap that place inside of her to alert her to what to do. She sighed, wondering if Lynx was right.

"Even though I am in a Murdoc shape, my whiskers are tingling. That isn't a good sign, Sarah. So you saw a sparkly light. That could be an enemy. Come, let's go back to this other way."

Sarah, glanced around, wishing she had some sort of vision or knowing of what the correct path is. She reflected on the conversation with Albagoth, remembering the genderless being urged her to trust Lynx. She moved her head to one side, "Okay, Lynx. I will follow you." She turned around and followed the retreating werecat back to the path she had veered off.

She wasn't sure where Lynx was leading her, but it felt right. It bugged her that she couldn't understand why it felt right, though. Sarah liked knowing why things worked. This was a new feeling, not understanding, but going along with it just the same.

Chapter 9

Sarah and Lynx made their way through old growth woods and vegetation that looked more like someone refused to keep up the fancy decorative gardens on an estate. In the distance, they could hear waves washing up on a shore and sea birds calling to each other. Sarah could see the birds in her mind's eye, dodging the waves, daring them to reach up and get them wet as they watched for fish or other delicious sea creatures. She smiled. It was humid, yet the atmosphere didn't feel right to be near a sea or an ocean.

"Do you hear the waves and smell the salt water?" she asked.

Lynx stopped in his tracks, lifted the human head, twitching his nose and chubby cheeks as if his whiskers were visible. "I feel moisture in the air, and light breeze on my whiskers. But the sea you are experiencing is an illusion. Albagoth cautioned me to be wary of the siren here named Shashamé. She is said to be the half-sister to the twin brothers who became the Wraith and the Fallen Savior. She thinks herself to be an oracle, like the old Greek mythos on your world of origin."

"It's just weird, Lynx."

"Yes, Shashamé is weird. Not sure how she heard about that Greek mythos."

"No, not that. I heard her once call to me, I think. I told her to go away."

"Oh. Then what's weird?"

"You in a human body talking about your whiskers is weird. Can you change your shape back to the form I'm most familiar with you in?" Sarah asked.

"No, not yet. I need to be in this shape to make it past the other Murdocs we will meet as well as the other groups that are opposed to your new rule, Sarah," Lynx, paused, sniffing the air, standing with his feet wide apart and arms up, with the staff held in a defensive position. Sarah sensed he was trying to make himself look bigger than he was. If he was in cat form, his fur would be standing on end.

"What is it?" Sarah asked, turning away from him, glancing around for herself, trying to sense what he was.

"Not sure. It's just too easy going this way. I sense there is something getting ready to pounce on us," Lynx turned around several times, narrowing his eyes.

"I don't think so. I can't feel what you do. Perhaps we just need to trust this and continue. This is the way you wanted to go, after all. But the smell of saltwater is getting stronger." Sarah held up her hands, palms upward as if catching the invisible water drops. "I can feel the water dropping on us. The breeze is bringing it to us."

"We must not go there, Sarah," Lynx hissed.

Sarah rolled her eyes, "Silly werecat, we'll be fine. Come on, follow me."

The air crackled and snapped like a lightning storm erupted during the hottest day of the summer. A bolt of lightning hit a nearby tree, snapping in two, opening a doorway to a beach with angry waves tossing and turning beyond.

"Shashamé, Shashamé, calling Princess Sarah and Lynx. Come on to my beach and we shall discuss all they you two are hiding."

Chapter 10

Xander marched ahead of Milo and Geoffrey, not sure where he was leading them. His thoughts turned around and around at how unfair it was that Milo and their griffin friend prevented him from going his own way. He wanted to explore this world and not worry about Sarah. After all, Sarah did make it clear she didn't need him to rescue her. He could hear Geoff and Milo talking behind him. Even though he couldn't make out all of what they were saying, he thought he knew they were discussing him and how angry and hard it was to get along with him. His eyebrows pulled down and the corners of his mouth pulled down, *I don't care what they think or say about me. It's time I realize I am a lone wolf. I can't waste my time worrying about what others think of me. I don't care that they are supposed to be my best friends and Geoffrey my protector. They violated my trust by making me stay with them. Albagoth, please guide me. I mean...*Xander's thoughts trailed off with a sigh. *I mean, I don't know what to do. Since we landed in this strange world, I feel lost and like your voice isn't reaching me. This world must not be one of the worlds you created.* Right after he said that, he felt a stab in his heart, like maybe he was wrong. Still he rationalized he had to be right.

Alexander Veh, you are treading on dangerous thoughts. Come to my beach. I will tell you what you need to know, a female voice spoke.

Who are you? He asked the voice in his mind.

Shashamé, the Goddess of the seas.

Milo spoke of you. Why couldn't Geoffrey see you?

I'm not meant to speak to him. Geoffrey is a myth on this world. Be careful. If either the Wraiths or the Fallen Saviors find him, they will put him to death next to the Lost Murdoc Princess. Right now, her life is in danger. You are opening yourself up to the evil one. Come to my beach.

I was heading there when Geoffrey grabbed me and made me follow him.

Are you a man or a little boy? What does your heart say?

Xander paused. If he was talking to himself, then why did the voice sound female? Indeed, what does his heart say? It says Sarah is on her own since she believes she can handle things herself. After all Healer Jaffrey gave her the magic bracelet and she opened the Shadowlands without his help. He let out a disgusted grunt. *I'm not needed at all. Sarah doesn't need me. I'm just a lost cause.*

"Looks like someone is feeling sorry for himself," Milo said, causing Xander to jump, looking over to see Milo next to him. "Sorry, I didn't mean to startle you."

"When did you come up beside me?" Xander asked.

"Long enough to get a sense of your dark thoughts. Geoffrey and I realized you're angry that we didn't allow you to follow the path we just came from. What we don't understand is why you are upset with Sarah. She is your love interest, right?" Milo jostled him.

Hearing that, brought a weak smile to Xander's face. "Well, sort of, but she and I could never be girlfriend and boyfriend. She's too tough and doesn't like being saved. She can handle herself. I can't tell her how I feel, Milo."

"So, you're just going to build a case of anger against her, ignore the fact that she could be in major trouble and go after that siren, Shashamé, right?" Geoffrey interjected.

Xander looked over to see Geoffrey was now on his left. They had him pinned in.

"Milo talked with her. Why can't I?" Xander protested.

"Because she might be leading both of you astray. I can't see her. If I can't see her, then that means there's something strange about this creature. I am a magical being," Geoff explained.

"And maybe that means you aren't meant to see her, Geoffrey. What if this world isn't one that Albagoth created? What if that means that this world doesn't have griffins and that could put you in danger. You are the one we need to protect. Not Sarah," Xander said.

"I call bull pucky on that," Milo replied. "I don't know anything about this world. But I do know based on what I learned when Albagoth turned me back into a human boy, that Albagoth created all worlds. I believe this is one the genderless being created, too."

"I don't," Xander whispered.

"Why not?" Geoffrey and Milo said together.

"Because I can't hear the Creator's voice in my being," Xander answered in such a small voice they couldn't hear him.

Back in his viewing room above the world, Ira watched Xander and friends walking. He saw the Indigo Traveler's dark thoughts. Ira rubbed his hands together. "My sister is right. This one has opened himself up to me. I can use him to snare that Lost Princess."

After he spoke out, he glanced around, expecting his brother to walk in. He heard something snap behind him. Nothing was there.

"I have to find a way to talk to that one alone. Perhaps he will assist me to trap that lost Princess. After all, if I read his energy correctly, he is already angry with her and doesn't think she will accept his help. Perhaps this princess is overconfident in her abilities."

A bright light appeared behind Ira and he turned to see his brother enter the room.

"No, brother, it is the opposite. Sarah doesn't know how to use her Murdoc magic that is inside of her. When it comes, it is haphazard and may end up hurting someone or herself. She hasn't been able to train with her Anansi because my followers have just captured her. They're holding her in some of kind of new cage inside a building."

Ira turned the screens to another side of their world to show Marshall, "No, she has escaped that. She let loose something that caused a massive destruction, knocking the head priest of your followers down. Some young kid helped her. Shashamé is leading them to her beach."

"Shashamé! I've told her to leave these Indigo Travelers alone! Especially the lost Princess. She doesn't know anything about her people. She was too young when she was moved to that human world," Marshall interjected. "I've got to get her out of there."

"No, Marshall. We have to wait to see what Shashamé will do."

Marshall shook his head and sighed with frustration. "You know she has the ability to cloud our viewers so we can't see what she's doing or hear what is said."

Ira leaned his head to one-side, "Yeah, that's true." He crumpled his lips in thought, "Actually, it's hard to read this Sarah, as you call her. And we must plan a way to make sure she doesn't take the throne. I mean, bring back the royal rule. It was abolished after my failed attempt to send you to the Black Hole. The Murdocs got rid of it to end the torture my followers and your followers did to them. But still that didn't work. We won't be satisfied until they choose a side and forsake their nature worship."

Marshall turned and shook his head as he turned his back on his brother.

"What do you mean, 'No?'" Ira's voiced sounded stern.

"Ira, we've lied to ourselves for too many years. We both know the true origin of our stories. We both know Albagoth is not truly our father. The creator of Worlds is genderless. Our father was a human and we are half-Murdoc, because Mom was full Murdoc."

"So what are you saying?" Ira approached him. "You're switching sides, aren't you? You're going to abandon your own followers, correct?"

"I already did. I tried to correct my teachings 200 hundred years ago. That's why they rebelled against me. That is why they beseeched you to send me to the Black Hole, tying me to that tree. Remember? It was Albagoth that rescued me, taking me up body and soul to meet in a realm far above all the worlds that was created. It was Albagoth that showed me how to create this realm so we can look down and monitor each of our people. We are not gods, Ira. We are more charged to be guardians. And not interfere unless we need to. With that said, we must find a way to peacefully unite the three paths on Wayla, thus helping Sarah bring peace."

"No! I am a god! I have not met with this Creator and I refuse to call it by a name!" Ira balled up his fists. "I also refuse to help this Murdoc Princess destroy my Wraith followers! She will make them stop being terrors of all the other two spiritual paths. She will make them become goody-two shoes, loving each other, loving pets and petty trees. They will become soft and gooey, mushy and fluffy! I won't have it. I will have nothing to do with it!"

"No, Ira. Your fear is irrational. She will allow each path to have their own spiritual celebrations. She will urge them to honor each other and honor the other paths, while not urging them to force the others to change. It is the way of Albagoth. After all, all paths lead to Albagoth and leads each individual to look within herself or himself. Just as I urge you to look within yourself to find your truth."

"I have darkness within me, Marshall! I've always been filled with darkness and that won't ever change!" Ira stomped over to the corner where his scythe was, grabbed it and marched to the door to get his cloak, which was hanging from a hook.

"Where are you going, Ira?"

"I have date with a lost Indigo Traveler!" Ira shouted.

Xander continued to be sandwiched between Milo and Geoffrey; he felt closed in, like he couldn't breathe. Glancing from one to the other, he stretched his arms out, knocking Milo in the upper arm. He had to raise his left arm higher into to slug Geoffrey in the shoulder.

"Hey! What was that for?" Milo rubbed his arm.

"Sorry, just stretching," Xander fibbed.

"You did that on purpose," Geoffrey accused. "You don't like us hemming you in. We don't plan to let you out of our sight."

"But you two don't have a plan. You two don't even know where we're going or how to get to where you think we need to be," Xander fired back.

"Grrr!" seethed Geoffrey.

"We will find Sarah by trial and error," Milo said. "The water goddess said this world is a maze and that pathways would open up without us knowing. We have to trust our instincts to know if the pathway that opens up is the one that will lead to the Murdoc village."

"Why do you want to go there?" Xander snarled.

"Because Sarah is most likely there. We have to hope she is, anyway," Milo answered.

"If she isn't, then she has been captured or is lost, like us," Geoffrey said.

Xander dismissed what his friends said, "She's okay. She can take care of herself. She keeps telling me that." Yet a small voice said he needed to be on alert and listen to them. He dismissed it, too.

A buzzing noise, like a mosquito, interrupted their conversation. They each looked around, pausing to look at the landscape closer. Geoffrey twitched his ear flaps, moving them one way and the other like antennae, to tune into the invisible information.

"Something isn't right," Geoffrey cautioned.

"That sound came before Sarah fell through a trap door earlier today," Xander exclaimed.

Milo narrowed his eyes, noticing the swirling of the air, like heat waves on a hot, summer day back home.

"Do we have any weapons?" Milo asked.

"I have my Dragon's Blood Sword. Crow Judge Connor allowed me to bring it with me this time. It's in my backpack," Xander replied.

"I have my talons and claws," Geoffrey said.

"I think we're prepared, then," Milo said, his skin prickled as his sweat glands went in to production.

"What about you, Milo?" Xander asked. "What do you have to fight with?"

"I have my ink pen. After all, the pen is mightier than the sword, so they say. I also have my ability to wish for stuff. If I touch the enemy, I can wish to bind him, and it will happen," Milo replied, stuttering a bit, because he wasn't sure if he could get close to whatever it was that would attack them.

Gears squawked and cranked, sounding like they needed oil. A tree and shrub parted ways, opening to a dark path with no light at all at the end of the tunnel. A hooded figure stepped through, holding a scythe. Milo steadied himself, doing his best to appear threatening.

"Ah, there you are, Xander. I've looking all over for you. Come a long, young one. I have good news for you. Or maybe I have bad news for you. It depends on how you take it," the figure said.

"He isn't going anywhere without us!" Geoffrey and Milo said together.

The figured laughed. "What do you two think you can do to prevent me from taking him? Milo, what are you going to do? Wish me to death? I'm Death, the bringer of death. You can't kill what is already dead, kiddo."

"I can try. Besides, how can you be dead, yet you stand before us, in solid form?"

"I have my secrets, kiddo. And you, griffin, you're an outlander. A being that doesn't belong on this world. If my followers capture you, they will put you to death. Your very life isn't supposed have been."

"I was created by Albagoth, like all beings," the white griffin defended himself.

"Not on this world. The being you refer to abandoned us eons ago. It abandoned you, too. No animals that look like you are here. Indeed, they aren't supposed to exist. I'm sure it pains you to be part, what, lion and eagle? Hmmm? Come on, kitty, tell the truth. Or is it, birdy?" Ira sneered.

"My nature is that of peace, whoever you are. I am one with who I am. How do you know our names and we don't know who you are?" Geoffrey snarled back.

Ira lifted his hand up to his mouth, smiled wirely, even though the boys couldn't see it, "Pardon me, I forgot to say who I am."

Ira tucked his scythe in the crook of his elbow, so he could clasp his hands together. The moment he did, a darkness surrounded him and began to creep towards the three boys. Thunder boomed, and a flash of lightning erupted.

"I am The Wraith! I lead all to the Black Hole where I prisoned my brother, the Fallen Savior!"

Milo and Geoffrey gasped. Xander laughed. They looked at him, puzzled.

"How dare you laugh at me!" the Wraith admonished.

"You're so dramatic! The Wraith is a legend on this world so clearly it isn't a real entity. Go away. Or tell us who you really are. I bet you're Lynx, trying to scare us, right?"

Ira's eyes opened wide at the same time he let out a surprised, "What? Who is this Lynx? Do you mean that stupid Snowshoe lynx that follows that so-called Sage of Stillness around?"

"Who?" Geoffrey and Milo asked.

"We aren't aware of the Wraith or the legend or even know who the Sage of Stillness is, either," Milo sounded puzzled.

Xander shook his head and shrugged, dismissing them. "No, not Manx. He's a real lynx. Lynx I'm talking about is a werecat – a shapeshifter. But he stays in the wild lynx form for some reason. On our home world, he appears as a Maine Coon."

Ira let out a frustrated sigh, realizing this wasn't going as planned. Setting his jaw, "Just come with me, Xander. These two fools don't know what's good for them. Once you are alone with me, I will explain to you who I am and show you I am not that foolish werecat you think I am."

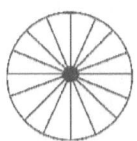

Xander glanced at Geoffrey and Milo with a wirily smile, "Yeah, sure I'll go with you. Besides, these two are hopelessly lost. Maybe you can point us in the right direction."

Xander walked forward and stood next to Ira. Ira grabbed his hand, smiling and laughing in victory, turned around, waved his scythe at the doorway, which opened and pulled the clueless kid through it.

Xander found himself in a dark, cold room with phantom lights flashing in different spots. He couldn't feel the person that pulled him through the doorway nor could he sense its presence. *I made a critical error.* Xander gulped some air. Taking a deep breath, he tried to get a sense of where he was. The small air smelled musty, and dusty, like it was flooded years ago and never was cleaned out. Clearing his thoughts, he listened intently for any sound. A twig snapped in near him, but too close. He took a cautious step, holding out one hand.

"Hello? Are you there, stranger?"

"Wraith. Call me Wraith. Bow down to me. Call me Master and your god forever more," Ira said, doing his best to sound like a demon.

"I will call you Wraith, but you are not my god or master," Xander spat. "Where the heck am I?"

"You are in my waiting room. This is the room I interrogate new inductees into my path. After you agree to my terms, I will take you to the Wraith Village to finish you training."

"Training? What kind of training? I haven't agreed to follow you or even admit you are anything but a person with a grandiose view of yourself!" Xander spat.

Ira glared at him, snooting hot air through his nose like an angry bull.

"Why is it so dark in here? I can't even see you or anything! I need light!" Xander yelled.

"Light is for my goody-two-shoes brother, The Fallen Savior."

"Ha!" Xander harrumphed. "I saw that weird statue of you two," he let out a chuckle. "The Sage explained it as if it was all real. It's legend. On my world there is a similar story of a man that was said to be the son of god. Little do you know, Albagoth created every world. Albagoth is genderless can't father children."

"Don't say that name! The entity was supposed to be my father! My Mother told us so and I believe her."

"Then you're just as deluded as everyone else," Xander snarled. "Look, I need some light. Next, I need something to eat and drink that symbolizing your blood and body of what you sacrificed for us, right? If you're a god, you can just make something appear out of thin air, right?"

Ira rolled his eyes, letting out a frustrated sigh.

"If I turn on the lights and feed you, will you listen to me?" Ira didn't understand what Xander was referring to, so he thought the teen was hungry.

"Maybe. I'm not a patient teen. I have a strange world to explore. I also have to discover why I dropped in this world."

Ira clapped his hands and the lights came on. "You're a fool if you don't know why you're in this world and need to be told."

"Okay I bite. Why am I in this world?" Xander crossed his arms and glared at Ira.

Ira shook off his hood so Xander could see his black eyes. "You're in this world because you had to play savior to that cursed Murdoc Princess. You're going to help me get her and punish her for coming back here. We need you to help us prevent her from taking the throne. She will destroy all I've worked hard to do."

"Why would I help you?" Xander asked, crossing his arms.

"Because you are angry with the nameless one for speaking back to you and forsaking you here. You've asked for guidance and get none."

Xander dropped his arms, stunned. "How do you know?"

"I see in your thoughts. I have the ability to read minds and see what you don't want me or anyone else to know."

Ira bluffed, but he could sense a little bit of Xander's thoughts.

Xander turned around, feeling like he just met someone just like him. "I used to be able to read people like that. I was taught to put up shields and now only read others when I have permission." He felt regret for not lowering his shields now. Maybe if he lowered his shields he could hear Albagoth again. Or learn to trust himself. He sighed.

Closing his eyes, Xander let go of his anger, choosing to forgive Sarah for her wanting to defend herself. The first thing he saw was his ego that was hurt when she opened the Shadowlands. And that it didn't matter who solved the problem. What mattered was making sure King Titus' soul was returned to his body, so he could finish his life. *I must apologize to her. Now to find out where she is.*

Remembering the lights were on, Xander opened his eyes, turned slowly around to see the room. The walls were painted a dark purple with small white dots that resembled stars. On the far side of it was a door with hand hold. The ceiling was high, about 100 feet high, like a skyscraper back home. *Odd. This room isn't meant to hold people. It's a passage way to somewhere else. It has to be. If he can read my thoughts, I must shield myself from him and figure out how to read him through it. Is he really who he claims to be?*

"You're not trapped here," Ira said, reassuring him. "You want some food, correct?"

"Yes. I realize gods don't eat, but I'm human. I'm very thirsty and hungry. So, can you just snap your fingers and a feast will materialize?" After he said that, Xander wondered if Milo could do that, too, even though he wasn't a god, either.

"No, I can't. But I can go get some food for you. I know which door will put me in the forest with the animals, vegetables and fruit." Ira approached a wall, waved his scythe and the doorway opened to him, he stepped through. Then back again, "Don't try to leave, human. I'll be back."

Now that he's gone, I must figure out who he is and what he really wants from me.

Xander's legs felt heavy, like he'd been hiking uphill for years without a rest. He took off his pack, dropped it on the floor and went over to a wall, then turned his back to it and slid down. Closing his eyes, he tried to visualize Albagoth as he saw the Creator two years earlier.

"Albagoth, not sure you can hear me in this world. I'm guessing you made this world—don't know what it is called. Please guide me. This Sage person told us about the Wraith and the Fallen Savior. I need more information. Sarah maybe in trouble, from what Milo said. Please show me how these two groups threaten the Murdocs. I haven't seen much of this place yet."

Letting go of his thoughts, Xander's breathing slowed, becoming even. He felt his spirit rise out of his body and float to another time.

He stood on the outskirts of a village bustling with activity. Little men and women, with large spiders carrying huge stacks of wood, fabrics and some with stones in baskets, crossed paths. Xander urged his spirit to move closer. In the center, he could see the village leaders, a King and Queen, helping with the building. Everyone was helping build a new room on the dwelling where the ruling family lived. Those who weren't building, were tending crops. Xander got closer, noticing each person and their spider had special tattoos.

Movement off to the side turned the workers attention. They paused to see what was coming through. A group of people dressed in various shades of purple and blue came through, singing hymns to the Fallen Savior. They came up to the workers and the royal couple.

"Greetings, Merrith," the Queen and King said, bowing from the waist.

"Greetings, King Davineh and Queen Aja. We come to tell you more about our Fallen Savior and the good news he shown us in our latest prayer vigil."

"I'm glad Marshall is still speaking with you after his fall," Davineh said. "We're busy right now. Albagoth shows us many things. And the trees are more than comfort to us."

"Bosh," said another follower. "The nameless one is incapable of guiding you all. Turn away from the false creator and hear the news of the Fallen Savior."

"He failed to bring you away from the heresy you all practice, worshipping trees and the Nameless One. But we take up his failings. He shows us the glory of the world to come with golden streets and rich waters that end."

"The Failed Savior forgives us our sins like we forgive him for not reaching out to you sinful Murdocs. We urge you because we love you, to come to him and renounce the false creator who would not claim his son."

A smaller Failed Savior, a child of about five, left the group and approached the workers. One of the young spiders went over to the child, lifted a front leg. The child took it, smiling.

"You're cute, Anansi. You have a drawing on your forehead. What does it mean?"

Xander moved closer to see what the child saw. It was a drawing of a tree planted firmly in the ground. He wondered about the spider being called an Anansi. He remembered hearing folktales of Anansi being a trickster.

"It means I teach other to root themselves firmly in the soil. At the base of a tree, we meditate, and we soak up the wisdom of the tree, as the tree teaches us about loving everyone, regardless of what they believe," the Anansi replied.

"That makes sense," the child said. "Do you have an assigned Murdoc yet?"

"Yes, but my Murdoc is working with the crops right now. What's your name?"

"I'm the One Not Seen," the child replied. "I'm too young to be noticed or to be listened." A tear fell from the child's eye.

"I am honored to notice you, Seen. I give you the name of Honor. If you ever want to be listened to, come to us."

One of the older Failed Saviors came over to them, took Seen by the arm and jerked her back in the group, saying, "Keep your filthy silk poopers away from our children!"

"Looks like they just noticed you," the Anansi whispered, sadly.

"Treat your children with love and respect and they will always return that love to you. But refuse to listen and allow them to show love to other living beings, like our friend, Sable," the King patted the Anansi on the head, "then they will turn their backs on you when they are of age to leave the village."

The leader raised his nose in the air, harrumphing, "We don't listen to Murdoc scum."

"If we're such scum, then why did you come to see us, brothers and sisters?" a worker said.

"We came to give you all the choice of joining us to praise and worship our beautiful Failed Savior or risk the coming to pass the loss of your first-born child," the leader said.

"Oh posh," the Queen pushed the comment aside with her right hand. "Our first-born child is eons away from coming. We don't fear Marshall's threats. We have our prophecy. The first-born child we bare will be a uniter of paths, Erway."

"Not if we can help it. If that child chooses to unite all of us, then we will join with the Wraiths to prevent that child from taking the throne. We will rid this world of your Murdoc threat before we abandon our Failed Savior. Where he failed, we will succeed. We can't fail twice!" Erway, the leader, said forcefully. He abruptly turned around. "Come, friends, let's leave this village."

Erway led his people away. The child stayed behind, staring at the unfinished dwelling. "What are you making?" she said.

"We're making a visitor's home for off worlders to come and stay. It will have many rooms and places for them to fix their food if they don't want to join us around our community fires for meals. It will have a room so they can meet and relax as well as individual rooms for them to rest at the end of the day."

"You all have drawings on your foreheads. Like me," the little girl held back her bangs to show she had a circle with a triangle in it. "I don't know what it means. But when my parents see it, it causes them to get angry. They say it has to go."

The workers and royal couple gasped in wonder.

"How old are you, Little One?" one of the workers said.

"I'm five, I think. I heard that the drawings aren't supposed to appear until I'm older. But none of the Failed Saviors in my village has them. So what will happen to me?"

"You are a very special person, Little One. It means you are a herald who will set the way for the first child of the new royal couple. Albagoth will prepare your heart and message. Be sure to spend time with the trees and near the water, to soak in the message."

"The water goddess lives in the water. I've heard to stay away from her."

"She only speaks to the off-worlders, Little One," explained the Queen.

"Not Seen! Come on!" Erway called.

"I better go. When I can, I will be back. I want an Anansi and to learn your ways." Seen said and then turned around to follow her parents.

Xander felt his spirit drawing away from that scene. Opening his eyes, he saw a new person standing before him, examining closer. This person wore a white robe, with the hood down, showing shocking white hair and piercing emerald eyes. His features were like the other man, except the other man had the blackest of hair and dark green eyes with a nose that was slightly crooked. Both men could be considered handsome, though, Xander wouldn't admit it. He knew Milo could say better, though.

"You need to leave here before Ira comes back. You're in danger," Marshall whispered, extending a hand to Xander.

"Ira? Who's Ira? And who are you?" Xander positioned his hands on either side of his rear and pushed his back up against the wall and then used his legs to push himself up against it more until he was standing.

Marshall cocked his head, giving Xander a puzzled look. "Didn't my brother tell you who he was?"

"He said he was the Wraith. I laughed at him, calling him Lynx. After all, the Fallen Savior and the Wraith are just myths, right? I mean we saw the statue and the Sage told Sarah and me the legend. But it can't be based on realty, can it? And if it was, you two should be dead. That was like 2,000 years ago, right?" Xander said.

Marshall pressed his lips together, shaking his head. Turning around slightly, he let out a frustrated sigh, wondering how he was going to explain this world to an off-worlder like Xander.

"It isn't that simple." Marshall scratched his chin, wondering how to explain this complicated world to him. "You three Indigo Travelers are tough nuts to crack. First the Lost Princess says I'm not all that great of a being and not worthy to be a god image! I mean, that gal should have been raised on this world! If she was, she would have known better than to kick a former god legend in the dangle-opters."

"She bruised your ego, too, eh? Sarah sure knows how to do that," Xander rubbed his privates. "See this bruise on my face?"

Marshall turned to look at him. "Yes, I see it."

"She slugged me a good one this morning because I woke her up from a nightmare. She isn't afraid to mouth off to anyone. I wish I was more like her."

"Ask her to give you lessons," Marshall suggested.

Xander, "Not a bad idea. Look, if you are Marshall, that means you're the Fallen Savior, right?"

Marshall nodded, glancing away, something struck him between his eyes. Narrowing his eyes, he looked at Xander, "You're a soul traveler, aren't you?"

"What do you mean, soul traveler?" Xander looked confused.

"Your soul leaves your body at will and takes you back to the past to view scenes. You saw some event in the past. Where did you go?"

"I- I- er- well," Xander paused, wondering how to explain this. "I don't know exactly. I went back to see what kind of threat the Fallen Saviors are to the Murdocs. I also wanted to see how the Wraiths threaten them, but my soul, as you call it, came back here. I woke – well—you know the rest."

Marshall nodded. "You saw the Murdocs building the Off-Worlder dwelling, correct?"

Xander nodded, "Yeah," he paused. "You were there, weren't you? So why didn't your followers recognize you?"

"Because they don't want to. They won't listen to me. They blame me for not bringing the Murdocs into their fold. The Murdocs aren't the threat."

"They aren't? Then who is?"

"It's about fear, Xander. I taught my followers to fear the Murdocs because they recognized the trees as having wisdom and being able to open the individual to the wonders of within. It's fear of knowing oneself and seeing Albagoth for the genderless wonder and creator it is."

"Albagoth, a wonder?" Xander drew out each word realizing the awe they brought. Remembering his experience two years ago, watching the genderless spirit appear to him in a swirling smoke entity, gradually taking a shape and the ease the being had to change form did cause the same excitement Marshall's words described. "Yes, you're right, Albagoth is a wonder." Then he thought about the trees, and how Sarah mentioned a tree in the Shadowlands helping her find her center and touch the unconditional love she used to open the Shadowlands. An "aha" moment struck him, "Sarah mentioned a tree last week while we were in Curá. I never thought about trees being like that, though."

Marshall smiled, "The tree awakened her to her Murdoc self. This is the quest she has needed all this time, Xander. She's on her home world. And she's in danger. In fact, your griffin friend is also in danger because he is part eagle and part lion. This world doesn't have any creatures like that, so the Wraiths and the Fallen Saviors will see him as an abomination. You need to come with me before Ira returns." Marshall again looked side to side and turning around as if looking for something. "Where did you say he went?"

"I didn't. He went to get me some food." Xander bent down, picked up his pack and walked into the middle of the floor.

"I know I should care about protecting Geoffrey, after all he has been my protector for two years. But right now, I'm more curious about this Wraith dude. You call him Ira. I still don't understand why they threaten the Murdocs and why they would hurt Sarah. This Ira, your brother, says he wants me to follow him. You say I'm in danger if I go with him, right?"

"Yes, because he plans to turn you against your friends and have you help him prevent Sarah from uniting the warring paths."

"But the Murdocs are peaceful. I didn't see anything about the Wraiths." Xander looked into Marshall's eyes, trying to see beyond the physical looks.

"Let me show you. May I touch you?" Marshall approached him slowly.

"Yeah, sure," the teen shrugged.

Marshall put his hand on Xander's shoulder, "Close your eyes."

Xander did, then felt himself being pulled back to the scene he just left. Except it was now night and the Murdocs were all tucked in their beds after a hard day's work. Xander saw torches at least hundred, coming down the paths. Some of the carriers of the torches moved them to the vegetation, lighting them on fire.

"We come to destroy all you have built!" the leader of the Wraiths called out. They came out of the shrubs and trees, surrounding the dwellings. "King Davineh, we call you out! Defend yourself. If you do not join us, renouncing the welcoming of strangers to this world, we will destroy your village. We will rape your women and children. We will put to death all you love including your precious Anansi! They are evil!"

"It is you who are evil, Dawanna," the king came out in his night clothes followed by his Anansi. "You welcome the darkness into your heart, renouncing all that Marshall tried to distill into your founder. Ira was misguided."

"We will send you to the Black Hole the way our evil Wraith sent his brother. You know the darkness is better than the light. Come join us and close the boundaries to strangers from other worlds. There is only Wayla."

"Albagoth created all worlds," Davineh's Anansi said. "We recognize that."

"Beware. Any heir to your Murdoc throne will be hunted down and destroyed. We will see to that. The Fallen Savior prophesied it and we share that prophecy. We also declare you to renounce your throne, and take up another form of rulership of your village. One that doesn't threaten us."

The king glanced to his Anansi, puzzled. "We don't threaten your way of life. We accept you and the other spiritual paths on Wayla. We recognize Albagoth created all paths and all paths lead to back to the genderless Creator of All Worlds. Because of that, we welcome travelers from other worlds. You all know the Sage of Stillness is from another world. He's been our first and main traveler. He has guided us to build this dwelling to welcome more travelers like him."

"We don't recognize the teachings of the Sage. We only recognize the darkness of the all-powerful Wraith! We renounce all paths that are different than ours."

"We accept you for who you are and say if your path brings you comfort, then continue to follow it. Please allow us the same courteous," the king said. "Good evening, Wraith followers. I must retire. Tomorrow is another busy day." He turned around, "Come on, Dancer," he said to his Anansi. They walked back into the royal house.

Dawanna growled in anger, "How dare you give us your wishy-washy blessings and then turn your back on us! We want you to shake in your boots and be very afraid of us!" He turned around. "Burn down the new building!"

His followers gathered around the new structure, threw their torches around it while singing praises to their Wraith, asking for the power of darkness to come and fill the Murdocs with fear and loathing.

Xander felt himself drawing back to his body. He felt anger, fear as tears weld up behind his eyes. As he came more aware of his surroundings, he felt the curious gaze of someone else. Opening his eyes, he saw a man with very black hair and deep emerald eyes dressed in a bright white robe with the hood down, watching him.

"You're in danger, Xander Veh. You need to follow me to safety."

"Who are you?" Xander asked.

"I'm the one who will keep you safe and reunite you with your friends, Sarah, Milo and Geoffrey," the man replied.

"How do I know you will? I'm waiting for the other dude that looks like you, I think." Xander said, then paused considering. "I'm not sure, though, because he keeps his hood up."

"We need to leave before my brother comes back. He means to lure you into his plot to keep the Lost Princess from the uniting this world in peace. You're vulnerable to his views because of you're building walls against the Nameless One. Come now, before he comes back," Marshall held out a hand to him too help him up.

Xander set his brow, drew away from the hand. "I can help myself up." He backed up further to the wall, drawing his feet under him and pushed against the wall to ease himself up against it. "I'm not going anywhere until you tell me who you are."

"I'm the one known as the Failed Savior. Others call me the Fallen Savior. I'm here to lead you to safety."

Xander rolled his eyes, "You've told me that many times already. Look, this Wraith fella is supposed to be bringing me food. I'm not going anywhere until I get something solid to eat."

Marshall took back his hand, uttered a prayer under his breath, as he considered what to do. "Do you value your friendship with Sarah?" he asked.

Xander thought of her enticing green eyes that sometimes looked blue or deep brown and the way she pulled back her blond hair and smiled. He sighed. He loved how she said his name, even when she was upset with him. But she was so strong and able to fight with the strength of a prize fighter. But she doesn't know when to allow him to protect her.

"Maybe she can protect herself," Marshall replied.

"What?"

"Sorry. After I was pulled into the Black Hole, the Nameless One gave me the gift of seeing what others think. I know I'm supposed keep what I know to myself, though. Just answer the question."

Xander set his jaw. "Sarah can take care of herself. She packs a powerful punch," he rubbed his jaw. Marshall noticed there was a bruise that was healing. "I rather stay here and learn more from this Wraith dude. You can leave." He bent down, picked up his backpack and turned his back on the Fallen Savior.

Marshall's face darkened with concern. Deep within him, he caught a glimpse of the changes that Xander would go through. "It is as you say."

The wall to the left side of Marshall blurred as Ira came back, carrying roots, a couple rabbits and jugs of water. He put them down when he saw his brother there.

"What're you doing here, Marshall?" Ira interjected.

"I've come to save your lost Indigo Traveler. I was sure he was being held against his will. But it turns out, he wants to be with you."

"There's other Indigo Travelers on Wayla. Go away and save them if you must! I going to feed my new follower." Ira dismissed him as he set the food and drink down.

"As you wish, brother," Marshall pressed his hands together and bowed slightly and then left through the wall in front of him.

Xander watched Marshall go through the wall, flooded with mixed emotions. Maybe he made the wrong choice. Slowly he turned around to face the Wraith, trying not to show he teetered on wishing he had followed the Failed Savior.

"Ready to eat?" Ira asked, inserting a skewer in the rabbit, sticking in the end in the ground and chanting a spell to cook it. He placed the root vegetables on skewers, too, and used the same flame to roast them.

Xander leaned his head to one side, "Aren't you going to give thanks to the spirit of the rabbit for giving its life so we may be nourished?"

"Why would I do that? Everyone knows these animals have no souls and exist solely for us to eat," Ira spat.

"Not everyone. Healer Astral taught us that all beings have souls. Even rocks and pebbles." An involuntary shudder climbed through his spine, shaking Xander. After he settled, he had a dread of what was to come. Still a little voice whispered to stick with this person or whatever it was.

"Healer Astral? Sounds like he spent too many years smoking that herb that supposedly helps you to tune into the outer regions dream realms," Ira twisted the rabbit, checking how it was doing.

"He was a griffin on the world of Curá and one of my teachers. His grandcub, Geoffrey is my friend and protector," Xander thought, then remembered he passed away a week ago and missed his wake. He choked back tears.

"Bah, griffins! Stuff of myths from other worlds. They aren't real, buddy. I don't know what you're playing with. Stick with me, I will tell you what's real. The Black Hole and my followers! We terrorize the Murdocs and all that represents the Nameless god. We punish those that worship trees and celebrate oneness in all forms. Currently, we are in high alert because the prophesied Lost Murdoc Princess is back on this world and we need to organize to prevent her from beginning a new royal lineage of Murdocs." Ira pulled out the rabbit. "Hot! Ouch!" he whimpered after touching it. "It's done." He handed it to Xander. The teen sat down on the ground, placing his pack beside him.

He took it, pulling off a leg, silently thanking the rabbit for giving his life so he may be nourished.

"Do you pray to root vegetables, too?" Ira chided. Xander's face reddened.

"What did Albagoth do to you that you refuse to say its name?" Xander asked after swallowing his first bite. "Do you want some?" he offered the rabbit back.

Ira shook his head, "No, I don't have to eat. My darkness keeps me alive."

"Okay," Xander drew out the 'a', "whatever floats your boat," he muttered under his breath. Speaking up, "Where are we going next?"

"Finish eating and I will show you." Ira stood up, glancing around the pure white space.

"What's this place called? This room?"

"This is the waiting room. It's where we take certain guests before we take them to our village. Only my brother and I know about it," Ira took down his hood, glaring at Xander with his startling dark eyes that didn't match is pure white hair.

Xander finished half the breast of the rabbit, and two of the root vegetables, but couldn't eat the rest. He burped, trying to remember his manners. Wiping his greasy fingers on his jeans, he burped again. "I can't eat anymore. Do you have a fridge to put the leftovers in?"

"Leftovers? What's a fridge and leftovers?" Ira dropped his stern tone.

"Leftovers is what a person can't eat and the fridge is a cold box that keeps them for later in the day so they don't spoil," Xander explained, picking up his backpack.

Ira kicked the dirt over the small fire, chanting a spell to extinguish it. After it was out, "I don't have such a box, but we can make such a thing." He thought for a moment, "Give me the leftovers." Xander handed them over. Ira muttered a spell and bubble filled with ice surrounded the leftover food. Once they saw how big it was, Ira knew they couldn't carry it, so he held it and muttered another spell shrinking it down to the size of river rock. He tossed it to Xander, "Put it in your pack." Xander didn't know what to make of what he just saw. He caught it and did as told.

Ira waved his scythe in front of the fall wall, opening the portal. They stepped through it. Xander heard a group chanting, "Wraith, wraith, mighty wraith, we gather to bid you be among us as we prepare to lay siege on the villages of the Murdocs and the Fallen Saviors. We seek your assistance to send them all to the Black Hole to meet you and know the awesome power and darkness you surround us all in. After we burn them all down, we will scour this land to find and destroy the legacy of the lost princess. Point us in the direction of where she is hiding."

Upon hearing his follower's prayer, Ira sighed heavily. "Oh, no! My followers do not listen at all."

Xander confused, stated, "I don't understand. I thought you want to destroy the Murdocs. After all, they freely say the name of Albagoth and worship trees. You burn down their villages and new dwellings for travelers who come here from other worlds." He remembered what he wanted to ask while he was eating, "What do you want with me?"

"You are my lure. You're the lost princess' love interest. She will come freely to us to save you. Also, your heart is dark. Your aura is a darker purple than most of your special breed of Indigo travelers."

"Love interest?" Xander choked. "What do you mean? Sarah and I are just friends. She can't stand the look of me and refuses to let me help her or protect her!"

Ira laughed, shaking his head. "You don't know the Murdoc women at all. They're usually stronger mentally, physically and emotionally than most Murdoc men. They also don't show their feelings as easy. I don't know human women because I wasn't raised on your world."

Xander followed the Wraith in silence, mulling over what Ira said. From the time Milo and Geoffrey found him, not counting what little bit that Sage fellow said to him while Sarah was zoned out, all he heard was about saving and protecting Sarah. He didn't understand why she was raised in the World of Nampa, a human world, instead of here. Nor did he understand why she became lost. He figured he couldn't lose anything by asking.

"Hey, Wraith, how did this Murdoc Princess get lost? Was she stolen from the king and queen?"

By now they were entering the group of followers chanting and communing with their god. Ira shook his head in disapproval. Hearing Xander's question, he turned around, faced him, taking down his hood.

"A long time ago, my brother's followers tested the legends of the Sage by hanging him from a tree. They were angry, disappointed and confused because he wasn't adhering to his own teachings by praying to a tree and he kept associating with Anansis. He even had a partner with one who continued to guide and counsel him. As he hung upside down, he proclaimed that the last heir to the throne would be born, thus breaking up the monarchy in the Murdoc way. Her life would be threatened because the other paths that my brother and I had formed, would know she come to unite us and bring peace to Wayla. We would be seeking to kill her to prevent that. So some unknown traveler took her to another world – his world--, after the king and queen used their magic to turn her DNA to human. The DNA would slowly convert back to Murdoc so by 15, she would find her way back here. Around 15 to 20, an etching appears on each Murdoc's forehead, showing them what their life's work is to be. The Lost Princess will start having dreams of this symbol and get snippets of what it means. She needs to be here to talk with the Albaohmen who will further guide her. I don't know what Sarah's symbol is, but I'm sure she has seen it in dreams and around someone who calls himself the Sage of Stillness. This Sage is an enigma and has been appearing on our world since my brother and I were young boys. In fact, he was quite close to my mother." Ira's voice cracked. He lifted a sleeve to his face to wipe away tears. "Now, we must attend to my followers and correct their misguided chanting." Deep within him, he saw a glimpse of Tomás telling him about the love a father has for his sons and remembered his brother's words of who their father really was. He felt a ping, of doubt about his own beliefs. He loved his mother, missed her, but had to continue keeping to his present course.

Xander's mind stood there, dumbfounded as many images and memories of Sarah speaking of spiders and pie type chart filling her dreams and nightmares and Xander remembered seeing a circular necklace around the Sage's neck. Only it didn't mean anything to him at the time. He felt torn between turning and running away or following. He decided he better stick with this death creature, or whatever he called himself. Though, his feet wouldn't move, like they had been cemented to the ground.

"Coming, Xander?" Ira turned to look at him. He raised his hood back up as he turned forward again.

Albagoth, please show me what to do. I realize this might not be in my soul's contract to be on Wayla. I thought we fell here by accident. I wish we had a Crow Judge to help guide us. Maybe I am angry that Sarah opened the Shadowlands. Maybe she knows something

*move about love and forgiveness than I do. Please allow
me to access the information I need to lead and guide
myself if you don't answer me.*

A small voice answered him, *Soul Xander. Look to
your soul and your lessons here. Forgive Sarah and see
meaning in what you are experiencing. Follow the darkness
before you can see the light.*

Ira approached Razbuator, the leader, "Greetings,
faithful Wraith worshippers. I have come back. I've never
died and continued to live eternally. I bring you a new
convert to our cause, Xander Veh, a traveler from the
human world." Ira turned to the whole group, which had
now quieted down to look at him. He held up his scythe
like a staff, "I also come to correct your misguided quest."

Razbuator frowned, glaring at the Wraith, "You again!
First you free our prisoners and the one we knew was the
lost princess and now you say our quest to destroy the
Murdocs before they build a new monarchy that will be the
destruction of all our way of life! You are not the true
Wraith! If you were, you would understand."

The crowd cheered, "Here, here." "How are we
misguided?" "Prove you're the real Wraith! How did you
create the Black Hole?"

"I didn't free your prisoners! They used their Murdoc
magic to break out!"

Ira thought back to when he was a teen, remembering
when his etching showed up. It was a large black hole. His
nightmare was of falling into a black hole and being
tormented by demons. Then one night, he saw he was his
own demon. He was tearing himself apart. A voice in the
dream said to become that which he was afraid of. Only,
there was a light at the end of the last nightmare. He saw a
glimmer of a white spirit whom would not reveal who he or
she was. Yet it spoke his name and said, "Wraith, you call
yourself. Wraith, you will be known by. At the end of 400

hundred year, you will meet the one you are most angry with."

Ira shook his head to hopefully shake out that haunting voice. Has it been 400 years? It seems like longer.

"The Black Hole always was here. I am a god, you all know this from the legends passed down from story tellers to story tellers. All I did was use my godly powers to reveal where it was. The location moves. It is not always by the tree the Failed Saviors hold sacred. Come, let us prepare Xander. He is the lure which we will use to draw back the Lost Princess. He is her mate."

"What?" someone shouted.

"How dare you come here and change our plans!" Razbuator snarled.

Ira faced him, "How dare I? I am your demon god! I am the one who issues and directs your quests. We need the Failed Saviors on our side. We need to convince them to help us in this way."

"How do you know the Lost Princess will come to us?" another shouted.

"Because she loves this weak human male. She has a soft spot for him and will go out of her way to protect him. Tie him up!"

"You lied to me, Wraith! You said you would teach me about darkness!" Xander shouted as the crowd gathered around him, gabbing his arms, roughly pulling his arms behind him while others tied scratchy hemp rope around his wrists. He fought and pulled back, only making the group more violent and rough.

Chapter 11

Sarah and Lynx approached the water with a mixture of curiosity and confusion. A large tide rose up, gradually forming a head, neck, shoulders, arms, with the body being the water.

"Shashamé calls Princess Sarah and werecat Lynx to her. They answer the call. Honored I am," said the water goddess.

"You're a siren," Sarah stated. "Not sure if I should trust you."

"Siren is a harsh word, Princess. I'm an oracle called to impart puzzles to each traveler according to what they have to figure out."

"Makes no sense," Lynx said, still in his Murdoc body, he lowered the staff he held.

"Lynx, you are a puzzle. You're a shapeshifter – preferring your Lynx form, but never comfortable being your true werecat shape. Why is that?" Shashamé inquired.

"Now is not the time for me to explore my own inner problems, siren. I'm here to help Sarah find Milo, Xander and Geoffrey. Albagoth sent me to make sure they get home safe," Lynx said. "When the time is right, I will shift back to my Lynx form."

Shashamé smiled, her eyes glistening in the sun's rays, "That form isn't your true form, either. Face yourself, Lynx." She turned to Sarah, "You think you know yourself so well, don't you?"

"I think I do, yes," Sarah replied slowly. "Though I'm concerned about many things this world has shown me and the dreams which I had planned to discuss with the leaders of the Murdocs."

"It will come in due time. For now, my dear, do you know who you really are? What species are you? What spiritual path do you adhere to?"

"What does that have to do with anything?" Sarah pulled away as if the water goddess was reaching out to touch her.

"It matters since you are charged with uniting this world in way that not everyone wants to be united. Are you a peace maker? The human world you come from is known for making war and fearing peaceful solutions. Where do you fall?" Shashamé inquired.

Sarah started to answer, "I-I," she paused, reflecting on all the images of war she saw back home including the movies in which killing was always the first resort. It used to bother her. Peace had to be the answer, she used to hear Milo and Xander say. Spiders are insects and look ugly, but the image of the Wraith beheading his brother's friend was uncalled for. Sarah shuddered. The Anansi's she met briefly were nice and offered to help her.

"I…peace. I stand for peace. But I can't be the one to unite these three paths. I'm an outsider. I have no Murdoc magic and don't have the training."

"It will come, Princess, when you are ready. I will open the way back to your village to finish your training and make sure to find your special tree to help you on your journey."

Sarah turned to leave, then remembered something. She remembered her anger and worry about why her human parents didn't tell her about being alien and why her Murdoc parents would give her up.

"Why was I sent away?" Sarah asked.

"That is a question for you to ask your birth father. Anger will keep you from completing your calling, Sarah. When you agree to it, your etching will appear and you will be united with your Anansi who will travel with you back to your adopted world."

"I don't know about going back to my adopted world, yet. I'm still trying to figure this one out," Sarah muttered. She turned around and started walking back the way they came.

Lynx turned to her, "Where are you going?"

"I'm done talking with the siren. I need to go back to the village of my birth. Are you coming, Lynx?"

Shashamé's smile spread. She raised an arm, held her hand palm outward and waved in a small circle, gradually widening it creating a vortex for Sarah go through. Lynx glanced at her with a questioning look on his face. "Go with her, Lynx. Shift back to the shape you're most comfortable with."

Lynx ran to catch up, just as he saw Sarah step through. He jumped right after her. When he came out, he landed on four feet and the staff dropping beside him. The thud startled Sarah, causing her to jump and turn.

Spotting the were-cat in his usual form, she ran back, picked him and hugged him, while he was still stunned.

"Put me down!" Lynx demanded.

"What? Oh, yeah! It's just, I'm so happy to see you in your lynx form," she let go.

Lynx sat up on his hunches lifted his front paws, turning them over back and forth, and spreading his toes, flexing them, to make sure each toe and thumb were still there. "I didn't shift to this on purpose. That water goddess made me change. I wanted to stay in the Fallen Savior form because I thought it would help us more." He sighed. "Okay, so do you want to carry the staff?"

"Me? No. Can you walk on your hind legs? If so, you can carry it. I don't want a weapon."

133

Lynx let out an amused meow. "The staff isn't a weapon. It's magical tool." He thought about it. "I supposed it could be used as weapon. But it could also help with peace."

Lynx stood on his hind legs and balanced. "I'm not sure about walking on my hind legs. I haven't done it before." He teetered back and forth.

"Do you want me to help you?" Sarah offered a hand.

"No, I can do it. Hand me the staff, please."

Sarah bent over and picked it and gave it to him. Lynx used it to steady himself as he walked forward. Gradually they went forward.

"Do you know where we are?" Lynx asked after a while, noticing more trees with markings on them, shrubs, flowers and other items.

Sarah listened. Not far ahead, she heard villagers chanting supplications to Albagoth. "We're near the Murdocs," she sounded relieved. "Come on."

As they approached, a Murdoc woman, dressed in armor made of hemp and man also dressed in a light armor came out. Beside each were their Anansis. Each had etchings of guards protecting the sanctuary. They held up staffs with ankhs on top.

"Halt, who approaches our ceremony?" the woman stated.

Sarah and Lynx glanced at each other, "Did you know there were guards here?" Lynx whispered.

"No. I wasn't here long before I was kidnapped by the Fallen Saviors," she whispered. She looked at the guards, "Hey, Nickoli and Jacca, and Petra can vouch for me. I'm the traveler, Sarah Johnson and this is my friend, Lynx, from the World of Curá. We side with the Murdocs."

"Sarah?" the man glanced at the woman, confused and unsure of himself.

The woman straightened up her staff, "Sarah, promised Lost Princess returned to us? Yes, we had a search party sent out to look for you. This world has become a maze. Come, welcome, Lynx from Curá."

They turned around, "Princess Sarah, you and your friend go before us."

Sarah and Lynx walked in front, the were-cat still teetering a bit, using the staff to steady him.

"I feel like a cripple," Lynx whimpered, consciously placing each back paw down and remembering how to use the staff to keep him upright.

"It's like a baby learning to walk, Lynx. You can do it," Sarah looked at him, smiling. "You are doing it. You walked just fine when you were a Fallen Savior teen. It isn't any different."

"It feels different," he grimaced.

Sarah considered that, "Maybe it does. I've never been a werecat, so I guess I wouldn't know."

Lynx chuckled good-naturedly.

They walked towards the gathered group, the Sage and Manx broke off and walked towards them. Manx trotted on, snarling and growling. He cornered Lynx, hissing and baring his teeth.

"Manx, back off. If he's with Princess Sarah, he's a friend," Sage replied.

"No, he's an imposter. He isn't really a lynx and yet it takes the lynx form. I will not have this abomination in this village!" Manx snarled.

"You aren't the leader of this village, Manx! We are guest teachers. Shall I remind you we are here to accept all beings, no matter how they present themselves?" Sage stately firmly.

Manx stopped snarling and hissing, hung his head, "No, Sage."

"Now apologize. If you can't be civil, go back to the gathering while I talk with Princess Sarah and her friend."

Manx turned around, tail tucked between his legs and slinked off. Sage watched him. Once he was gone, he turned back.

"Sarah, where did you go? Your training was supposed to start a day ago," Sage said with concern.

"I was kidnapped by the Failed Saviors. Lynx, here, is a werecat, he shifted into the image of one of the teen followers and helped me escape," Sarah motioned to Lynx.

Sage acknowledged Lynx's action with a head bow.

"It wasn't me, Sarah. You used an explosive of some kind. I didn't see you throw it, but it packed a punch," Lynx replied.

"Explosive? Tell me more," Sage urged.

Sarah lifted her hands up as if she was surrendering, "I don't know what I did. I was listening to Thomas –that was the name I gave the boy – drone on about the history of the Fallen Saviors. My mind traveled back to sitting in science class listening to my teacher talk about atoms and molecules interacting. An image of them dancing and moving together in waltzes formation that became more of a mosh pit as they collided with each other at 1000 miles per hour, causing a mushroom cloud. Next thing I knew, the blast rang out, waking me up. The jail door was blown off and the far wall knocked down, landing on the Failed Savior guard who was questioning Thomas – err—Lynx. We left. I don't know what happened."

Sage, speechless, glanced around, turned slightly, then closed his mouth, looking at Sarah from the corner of his eye. "Come, we need to get you to your birth father and another Albaohman for training. We will also match you with your Anansi."

Sarah's eyes met Lynx's. Her heart dropped, she wasn't sure if she did something wrong or had illness. She sputtered as she ran to catch up.

"Did I do something wrong? Or do I have illness?" She asked. "Before Lynx changed to his normal form, he said I used Murdoc magic. What does that mean?"

"You will learn, your Highness," Sage walked with purpose.

The chanting stopped as they approached. Sarah looked at each one.

"What's going on here?" she asked. "The village looks like it's preparing for something."

"Our seers have alerted us the Failed Saviors and Wraiths will be joining forces to march on us. We need to prepare. Time is short, Sarah. You've only been here for a short number of days and haven't had time for training," Albaohman Quay said.

"There is time," Sage replied. "Davineh? Where is Davineh?"

"There's no time!" Quay insisted.

"We will make the time!" Albaohman Davineh, a small, stout man, but he held himself with authority, came forward. "Sarah, I'm your birth father. I'm sure you have questions as to what happened, but there's no time for that. I sense you have had an experience—an awakening to your gift and magic?"

Sarah felt a tug in her heart. He looked familiar to her. Like she's seen him before. Eyes, eyes have it. He had her eyes. Or maybe she had his eyes. If that was true, then wouldn't he be blind? Sarah shook her head, *I must be tired and hungry.*

_"Um, I guess I did." Sarah wasn't sure. Her mind flooded with images of the circles with the many divisions, the voice calling her to unite the divisions and the explosion. Closing her eyes, she couldn't decide what to say first.

Albaohman put a hand on her arm to steady her. "How old are you, Sarah?"

"I'm fifteen. I'll be 16 in two months."

"It's time you knew," Davineh took her by the hand and led her out. He summoned an Anansi to follow them. Lynx, concerned about where he was leading her, dropped the staff and followed.

Albaohman Davineh turned to him, "No, werecat Lynx, this is not for you. She is safe. I know Albagoth sent you to look after her and the other Indigo Travelers. You all will be united in time. This is Princess Sarah's sacred journey."

Lynx paused, "How did you know my name? Sarah didn't introduce me."

"I'm leader of the Murdoc. Would be king, and spiritual head of the Albaohman, but it was forced to disband when the Fallen Savior failed and issued the prophecy. As lead Albaohman, I see what others do not. I see your true form, Werecat Lynx. It is a wise form that you aren't comfortable with now. Your own journey will approach when you will join with others to explore this. But now is not your time. Sarah will be fine."

Lynx's fur puffed out, he lifted his jowls and let out a low hiss mixture with growl. Sage reached out to him, soothing him, Lynx looked up at him, and eased up, realizing that the Murdocs didn't mean to hurt him.

Davineh lead to Sarah to another opening with a few sturdy trees –mixture of oak, weeping willows and birch. Sarah spotted a Banyan tree over by itself. *That's odd*, I *wonder why it is the only one.* An Anansi caught up to them.

"I'm here, Albaohman Davineh," he said.

"Sarah, this is Nickoli. I don't think you've met yet. He is the one I believe you will be matched with."

"I think we've met. I'm not sure," she remembered uttering his name a few minutes ago, but now wasn't so sure. "You don't have one of those drawings on your forehead. But neither do I. I don't understand," Sarah felt puzzled.

"Many things have to happen before it appears. First you need to understand why we chose to give you away. What do you want to know?" Davineh appeared confident and patient.

Sarah thought back to when she was in the Shadowlands, angry, confused and wishing her parents had told her the truth. Her oldest brother always said she was from a different planet. "I thought I was human. Raindom, a Banyan tree I meet a week ago, said I was part human and part Murdoc. Now I heard I am full Murdoc and my genes were disguised as human. Why did you all take me to the human world?"

"You would've been killed if you stayed here. I am descendant of the kings and queens. We disbanded the monarch after Marshall was hung from the tree. Our monarchy never saw itself as better than the common people. We all worked together, so it was easy for us to change our democracy to a more community setting. We knew when you came along, you would change the rule, slightly, but be able to unite everyone in a way that we could not.

"To answer your question, your etching will come after you find your special tree, ask it to be your tree and show you what you need to do to unite the fractions. Nickoli will assist you."

"I guess that's okay," Sarah flicked her fingers on both hands, glancing at the ugly spider next to her.

"I'm sensing you are already seeing visions and have a symbol appear to you," Albaohman commented, putting a hand on her shoulder.

"I see the image of a small circle within a larger one and many divisions or paths there. This is the same image that the Sage or Tomás wears around his neck."

"Tomás? How did you learn his real name?" Davineh eyes opened wide.

"At the statue. I saw the story of the life behind the Fallen Savior and the Wraith. Only I'm not sure why the Wraith is so angry and why he won't believe he has a human father."

"Interesting. Do not tell anyone else his true name. Yes, you are beyond ready. Your etching will begin to show up within the next day or so. Now, Sarah, go find your tree."

Sarah agreed. Glancing around, she headed for the Banyan tree.

"No, use the Birch," Nickoli urged.

"Allow her to choose. Once she has settled herself, you go beside her and watch her journey."

Sarah glanced back at her birth father and new friend. *Nickoli is different than I thought he would be,* she mused as she headed for the Banyan tree. *He's still ugly, but there's something familiar about him.* She approached the tree and snuck another look at her Anansi, wondering how something so large, hairy and creepy looking could be useful to her. Flashes from the vision at the statue reminded her how those Anansis guided their people. She took a deep breath, let it out slowly as she braced herself.

"Hello, Banyan tree. You remind me of Raindom," Sarah whispered, placing her hand on the bark. She glanced down, noticing the saplings around her crawling towards her, lightly wrapping their young branches around her like a young child welcoming a parent who returned home. "Do you have a name?"

Names are for the living, young Indigo Traveler from the adopted world of Nampa, the tree stated.

But you are living and you have young ones to nourish and mentor.

True, but my time is due to go to the beyond and seek a new beginning. For now, I'm here to give to you. What is it you need or want to know?

Sarah thought, glancing back to see if Albaohman Davineh was still there. He wasn't. But Nickoli was now closer to her biding his time. *I'm not sure. I need to be trained in what to do. This world is still new to me. I don't understand why I was taken to another world. I don't understand what is expected of me. I don't feel Nampa is my true home and my parents that are raising me lied to me. Why do the Murdocs here expect me to become their savior? They put such faith in me, but they don't know me.*

There's so much I don't know.

Sarah paused, took a deep breath and let it out, hoping to still her mind. She hadn't learned to meditate formally, so she really didn't know what to do. She heard a deep, rough voice inside her mind speak, *Extend your roots down to the ground, like I am doing.*

Roots? I don't have roots.

Imagine, your highness.

Sarah squeezed her eyes until they hurt but heard the soft gruff tone to relax and not try so hard. As she let go, her legs started tingling and sensation of being pulled down into the ground at the same time of being pulled upwards tugged her spirit.

Good, now focus on my bark. Open your inner eye and see the doorway open into me. Once in, you will meet my spirit and know the guidance you seek.

Sarah wasn't sure what the tree meant by inner eye, but she let go of guessing and just went to the area between her eyebrows. A slim branch lightly touched that area opening a brilliant golden light within it were sparkling blues, purples, pinks, and oranges. At the center, a door opened and she felt her spirit being pulled towards it. The door opened before she reached it, a glowing image of a tree waving to her with one branch and extending his other branch out to grab her hand. Once she reached him, holding his hand, her feet touched inside the entry way.

Welcome, Princess Sarah. I am Waylon of the Banyan Wisdom trees. We can be found on most worlds that Albagoth, the Creator of All Worlds has made. Yet few Murdocs chose us to meditate and bond with. You are the chosen and it shows because you were drawn to us. As it was foretold long ago."

I don't know why I keep being called Princess. I hate girly things and desist dresses, skirts and pho-pho stuff like that. Give me my black Tripp pants, black army boots and black shirts or an orange and black-tie-dye shirt and I'm soaring in the skies.

Waylon's leaves rustled, shaking all his branches. Sarah realized he was laughing. She also sensed he didn't understand fully.

I may not understand the way you intend it, but I understand on another level. You're a rebel on your world. You are a rebel and an outsider here, too. Even though this is your world of origin. Come, you will begin your training and be shown why you are the new crowned royalty of the Murdocs.

Chapter 12

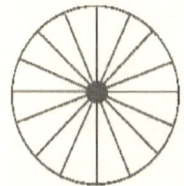

Sarah followed Waylon, wondering how her training would commence. Would be given a weapon, the way Xander was given his dragon blood sword? Would she learn hand to hand combat or something else?

She remembered is a meditation or sorts, so she wasn't sure what to expect.

Waylon paused, turned to her, drawing in his branches, *We begin.* He moved one group of branches up to above his head and the other group down to ground while saying, *Mystery is all around us, Princess Sarah, we trust Albagoth, creator of all Worlds.*

Those words sounded familiar to her. She vaguely remembered that monk or Sage coming to the cage she, Petra and Jacca were in a day ago. She knew she was supposed to say something but couldn't remember what.

Listen to me, you will learn what to say, Waylon redirected her.

Who leads us all to the path that best suits us. And all paths lead everyone within themselves. Waylon's branches moved in a smaller circle, then formed a larger one and then made six or more separate lines toward the smaller one. Sarah remembered the monk doing that, too.

Albagoth has passed down these words from eons to eons across the galaxies. We are already whole. We are our own savior. So be it, in the name of all Good and all Oneness, Waylon finished.

So I'm supposed to travel within myself to find the right path for me?

Yes, your highness. You have begun your journey by stepping inside. What I have just recited is the prayer of knowing that all Murdoc use in their celebrations of Albagoth. There is another which speaks of the acknowledgement that all life is conscious and worth preserving. You are tasked with imparting this to the Failed Saviors and the Wraiths, while affirming they are valued and do not have to merge with their Murdoc brethren. But they do need to live in peace with them.

How am I to do that? Don't call me princess! I can't be one.

You are the first of the new royalty. It will be explained. Silence your mind, Sarah.

Sarah saw herself sit down, calming herself within the vision. Waylon and the glowing room faded away to darkness as she pulled along a dark tunnel with flashes of lights like many cars zooming at warp speed past them. The darkness and lights lifted, dropping her in a lush green meadow surrounded by flowers of every shade of color and every shape. In the distance, she heard voices calling. She went to voices, noticing they were gathered around a fire, holding a baby. The queen and king, wearing crowns of the wild flowers, dressed in common tunic and leggings, like five others, comforted the little baby. Behind them was a hut, built of stones and mud. The Sage of Stillness and another Murdoc came out.

"Yes, Rayon, the new leader of the Failed Saviors, said he stands with the Wraiths. If we keep her, they will kill her so bring doom to them. They fear she will force them to give up their way of life," King Davineh, his face showed the pain and worry he felt.

"Even though we know that won't happen. She's a uniting of all. I will keep her safe. Did you write a note for her new parents?" Sage asked.

"Yes, but it won't be in a language they understand. You take her to your human world, correct, Tomás?"

"Yes. To the World Known as Nampa. Albagoth lead me to a family that will raise her well but won't know she's from another world. I have a contact with human services who will assist me."

The queen handed the baby over. "What is her name?" Sage asked.

"Serena," the queen cooed.

The Sage towered over the Murdoc people, standing a good six feet two, compared to their two feet five inches. As most people, Murdocs are variety of heights, though, some are taller and wider.

The baby sucked her small fingers and cooed back her mother.

All the adult Murdocs gathered around, gazing at the royal infant.

"Did you do the spell to disguise her DNA?" Sage asked.

"No, not yet. We have concerns about her not ever returning to us or that her etching won't come at 15 or that she will never know she isn't human," the queen and king said almost together.

"Reasonable concerns, your highness." Sage. He handed the baby to the smaller Murdoc man who looked like he was a nanny, since he wore simple tunic, an apron and had a ready bottle to feed the baby with.

The Sage paced away from them, stroking his chin. Turning around he said, "Albagoth will find a way to make sure she returns. It will be programed into her altered DNA. As it wears off, it will trigger her spirit to return. Especially if she bonds with a tree of the wisdom species during her 15th year. Once that happens, it will trigger a homing signal to bring her here. After her full training, her etching will begin to appear." Sage said.

Sarah felt herself drawing out, still hearing the echo of what happened when she was a baby. More questions arose, as she wondered why she grew taller than her birth parents and was thinner. Perhaps it was because they altered her DNA. As her spirit withdrew, she could hear the Sage muttering the spell to change her. The next scene she saw was the Sage, now dressed in jeans and polo shirt of the common people of the World of Nampa of the early 1990's, to her adopted parents. She heard him say the baby would be more advanced in some areas and they would have to learn to adapt to her. He urged them not to hold her back or treat her different than their other children. At that time, they only had her older brother, was barely three years old. The young boy ran up to them, and mentioned her weird ears, shaped like albino broccoli.

"Jarrod, that's not nice!" his mom corrected him.

"But's it's true," the young boy pouted. "I hate albino broccoli! I don't like her, either! Why couldn't the alien be a boy?"

"Son, that's enough! Sarah is not an alien. She's a human," his dad said sternly.

His mom looked at the stranger, noticing he wore a gold chain with a circle with many divisions that lead to a smaller one. Leaning her head to one said, she said, "That's an interesting necklace you have. I've never seen anything like it. Where did you say you're from and who were her birth parents?"

"They're from another part of world," Sage said. "The necklace is one I made for myself. It will also have special meaning for your new daughter. The paperwork is all legal, Mr. And Mrs. Johnson," he took out the paperwork from a knapsack by his feet." He handed the forms to Mr. Johnson.

"White broccoli ears!" Jarrod poked the baby.

The baby turned her head, opening her eyes, looked right at him and stuck her tongue out at him.

"Mom! She stuck her tongue out at me!"

"Jarrod, she's a baby! Stop poking her. If you can't behave, I'll send you outside."

Sarah laughed her spunk even back as a baby. Her spirit pulled further away, going down a long black tunnel, pausing and abruptly she felt herself jerking back and then yanked upward, sending her sensations into panic mode. Once her spirit reached the furthest star, it paused, as she heard some being calling her name.

Sarah, come. Sit down and review what you have seen and heard.

Who are you? She asked, glancing around.

Don't worry about my name. You have questions. I will lead you to go deeper within. No more reviewing the past. See only what is inside yourself.

I hate being alone with myself. She thought again. *Maybe I do like the solitude, but when I am, all I feel is like I don't belong in Nampa in that world. And this one is still new to me. I feel so at odds with being a princess.*

Sarah, allow those questions to float free, focus on deep within yourself, asking your Soul for direction.

Aren't I supposed to look to Albagoth to direct me?

A deep rumble shook her being, she realized whoever was talking with her was laughing.

I don't understand. Are you Albagoth?

I am a spirit entity that works with Albagoth. We're directing you to get your answers from deep within you, as all Murdocs do. And some humans, as well. Quiet your mind. Ask your soul for direction.

Sarah did as directed, taking a deep breath and letting it out slowly, she felt her body and spirit essence further relax, brilliant colors of every shade burst out, forming a kaleidoscope of patterns, shapes, doing a dance and flight of images. They broke into groups. The indigo group formed a large circle, a smaller deeper purple group formed a smaller circle within it, while groups of yellows, reds, blacks and blue and various others formed lines to the smaller circle. In cursive Sarah saw the words, "All paths lead to Albagoth. All paths are equal. Albagoth leads all paths to go within."

In a larger print, she read and heard a voice say, *Sarah, your task is teaching others to go within, accepting all where they are at.*

Gradually, they faded out. She still didn't understand.

Sarah saw herself standing in a meadow. Beside her was the Banyan tree, Waylon. Another Sarah stepped around and stood in front of her. The other Sarah drew the pattern on the ground, which formed a three-dimensional emblem. She heard up a finger, pausing the question Sarah wanted to blurt out. Then the other Sarah jumped inside her.

She felt whole – understood—wanted to follow, what did the other Sarah want to show her. How is this part of her training?

Her eyes flew open. Waylon boomed a *hello,* startling her.

Did you have a nice meditation? Waylon asked.

"Give me a minute," she said, drawing out each word. "I felt like I was on some kind of a drug induced trip." She rubbed her eyes. The tree rumbled his leaves. "I don't understand. I mean- I saw myself or someone like me jumping inside me, and I wanted to follow her. I wanted to know what she meant and what I was supposed to do. How are all those strange things going to train me?"

Hmmm. Perhaps you need to let it sit for a while. Walk around and see the Albaohmen. Talk with your Anansi, Nickoli.

Sarah, knitted her brows, frowning in consideration. Turning to Nickoli, she jumped, not expecting him to be right there.

"Sorry, Sarah," Nickoli extended one of his front legs to bow, keeping his front four eyes on her.

Just looking at him, made her skin crawl. A sparkle of gold glittered off of Nickoli's forehead, she looked closer, noticing an etching was revealing itself.

"Nickoli, you're getting your etching. What does that mean?"

He put up a leg and felt it, smiling. "It means you will be getting yours, too. Come, let's walk and talk about what you noticed."

Sarah agreed. Something began to change within her.

Silently, the two strolled down a meadow. Sarah reflected on her visions and the tree. "Oh, my heck! I forgot to thank Waylon for helping me. But I'm not sure what conclusions I've come to."

"What do you mean?" Nickoli said.

Glancing around, "I mean, how am I supposed to unite the two spiritual paths here? I still don't understand how they practice their faiths. It seems to me, all the Failed Saviors want to do is convert the Murdocs to their way of thinking or kill them off in order to forget where they came from. And the Wraiths are just angry that the Failed Saviors chose good and angry because they want Albagoth to approve of their deity, the Wraith, is his son," Sarah looked over at Nickoli.

"That's about right. What about you? What path do you follow?" Nickoli asked, showing her a down log, "Have a seat, Princess. We can talk more."

Sarah thought of the circle within the circle and many paths that lead to the smaller one.

"I don't want to be called Princess. Where I was raised, princesses were all girly, wore pink and acted like spoiled little brats, expecting others to wait on them and be treated like they were fragile."

"You will re-introduce the new monarchy, though. You will begin a new kind of rule, while bringing in your own way of doing it," Nickoli reminded her.

Sarah shook her head, "I want to go back to my world and finish school. I want to change the world, and have my rebellion open doors. . ."

"That starts here, though."

"Maybe. But I'm only 15 and this world is still new to me. How am I supposed to get the adults here to see what I know and follow me, an outsider?"

Nickoli nodded his head, "Good insight. Do you believe in yourself? What do you believe in spiritual views?"

Sarah lifted one shoulder up as she tossed his words around. Pursing her lips, she let out a soft humming sound, considering what to say.

"I know how to fight. I believe I can hold my own with anyone who wants to take me out." She scratched her ears, noticing they seemed to be getting bigger, or something. A bird a flew by and a few small insects.

"You aren't answering the question, Sarah. Do you know Albagoth created all worlds?" Nickoli redirected her.

Sarah raised her eyebrows, looked up and round, noticing the sun filtering in through the clouds. A slight breeze blew. They heard running feet and noticed the sunlight reflected off many fine silk threads.

"I met Albagoth a few days ago. I doubt Xander knows that or would accept them. I have been told Albagoth created all worlds and I do believe it. I just don't know how to go within. The vision showed me as a baby and what happened – oh my heck, the Wraiths and the Failed Saviors are all part human, right?"

"Yes, they are—but why does Xander need to know about your visit with Albagoth?" Nickoli looked closer at the threads, noticing they were moving. Sarah shrugged. "Someone's coming. First, to go within," he touched her belly button, "focus on the area above your belly button. Close your eyes."

The indigo teen followed directions, relaxing. She traveled back to the meadow where her double jumped inside of her. She saw herself in the center of the of the larger center, walking on one of paths away as if she was on a tight rope. As her double walked, the path became a large meadow with many shrubs, wild flowers and vegetation as well as stubby trees. As she walked through, she heard a boy's voice calling for help. Emerging, she saw Xander tied to a tree with Failed Saviors and Wraith Followers guarding him.

She overheard them say, "When she comes, we will pounce on her, knock her out before she can detonate one of those Murdoc bombs,"

"Murdocs don't have bombs! What's a bomb?"

"Someone shut that boy up!" another shouted. A guard closer to him backhanded him across his mouth.

Coming out of the vision. She heard another voice say, You will know what to do. Albagoth and many other spirits are guiding you. You are guiding you, too."

"Xander is in trouble! We have to go to him!"

The running feet stopped by their log, "Princess Sarah, Nickoli, the Sage of Stillness, Manx and others need you! Your friend and fellow Indigo Traveler is being held prisoner by the Failed Saviors and Wraiths!" Said one Murdoc boy. His Anansi landed by him.

"And a griffin and another traveler just reached our village." Another girl said, both struggled to catch their breath.

Nickoli clicked his two legs together, growing, "Jump on, Sarah, we're going to swing by my threads!"

When he stopped growing, he lowered himself so she could climb on. The Anansi began muttering words Sarah couldn't understand, she could feel him moving his back legs as if he was climbing a rope. Turning around, she saw he was pooping out thick silk threads, pulling and weaving them together, his back legs working foot over foot as quickly as he could. Once he had enough, Sarah's mouth fell open she watched him maneuver the rope, forming a

151

large loop, like a lasso, tying a knot and then passed it forward to his front paws. He gripped it, "Duck!" Sarah followed his orders. He raised it high, and swung it, circling overhead as fast as he could and then aimed for the highest branch on the furthest tree, landed on the end of it and Nickoli pulled it to the middle of it, and yanked it tight. Sarah, facing forward, felt awed by his expertise to maneuver his thread like that.

"Hold on tight!" he said again, at the same time he sprung from the ground and swung his body up and managed to send another thread to the next branch, like Spiderman. Nickoli cut the threads behind him.

It reminded Sarah of being on one of swinging on the monkey bars in elementary school, only they were going at lightning speed, and she heard a swooshing noise as they whipped from branch to branch. She could see more Anansis swinging beside and behind them.

In a matter of minutes, they arrived close to the village. Nickoli and the others dropped down with the agility of a cat.

They scurried along about twenty yards when Milo and Geoffrey came up to them, shouting.

"Sarah! You're on a spider! You're facing your fears!"

"Milo! Geoffrey!" she jumped off Nickoli and ran to them as they ran to her. They collided in the middle, wrapping their arms around each other. Geoffrey stood up on his hindlegs, put one front paw on Milo's shoulders and another one on Sarah. After a couple minutes, they separated.

"We have to find Xander! He's in trouble!" Sarah said.

"The spider! You're afraid of Spiders, yet you were riding one," Milo said, as they walked back, to the center of the village.

Sarah noticed the Sage of Stillness standing with others from the village. The Sage broke off from them and began to walk with purpose toward them.

Turning to Nickoli, raising a hand to motion for him to hurry to catch up, "This is Nickoli. Nickoli, this is Milo and Geoffrey. Milo is from my world and Geoffrey is from Curá," she introduced.

"Pleased to make your acquaintance," Nickoli tipped his head to each one. "I'm Sarah's Anansi partner. I will be guiding her and mentoring her in your spiritual growth, wisdom and be the confidant she needs through life."

"I see," Milo drew out each word, still not sure what to think. He noticed a speck of dust or a spot on, Sarah's forehead. He lifted a finger to wipe it away. Sarah backed off, striking his hand, not sure what he was doing.

"What was that for?" he yipped.

"Why were you going to poke my eye?" she snapped.

"You have a speck of dirt on your forehead."

"Uh . ." Sarah glanced at Nickoli, noticing his etching growing larger. Her Anansi smiled.

"Yours is materializing, too, Princess," he said.

"Don't worry about it, Milo. I'll explain later."

"How do you know Xander is in trouble?" Geoffrey inquired, glancing from her to the path.

"I can't explain it," Sarah shrugged, reviewing all the visions and things she learned. Yet there were still a million questions revolving in her mind and subconscious. She posed a simple request to sneak some time to herself to explore what they mean, hoping to find answers.

Sage, approaching closer to them, greeted them with eyes open, then narrowed them as he observed something was wrong. Leaning his head to one side, he scrutinized her, "You know Xander's been captured. We must go. I want to know how your training went, but that will come later. Come, let's gather the forces to get him."

Raising her hand, "No, Sage, I don't think that is wise. Wraith is among the group. It's joint effort with the Failed Saviors. Wraith trapped him and it is a trap for me, too."

"How do you know, Sarah?" Milo asked.

"I saw it in my last vision."

"Are you going alone?" A new voice asked.

Sarah looked over to see her birth father, Albaohman Davineh standing there with Manx and Lynx.

Sarah glanced away, looking at the trees, searching for the right answer, wondering what the best way would be to deal with this.

"I don't know. I don't know how to fight two whole villages. I'm only one person. But if I go alone, then I risk my own life. I know there is a bigger plan. I escaped one jail cell by daydreaming about atoms and molecules colliding causing an atomic explosion only to have break through the bars and blow out a wall, almost killing Lynx in the process. I'm confused, and yet know I have to do something."

"You're Murdoc magic comes natural to you but you don't know how to channel it. It still has to be honed and directed," Davineh comforted.

"I guess so. What's the best way to handle rescuing Xander?" Sarah asked.

Milo, Geoffrey re-positioned themselves to Sarah's side, looking at Sage and Davineh. In turn, they glanced at each other.

"We go to the village wisdom tree, call on Albagoth and seek a group wisdom quest to discern the best way to handle this," Davineh says.

"No, we don't have the time," Sarah replied. "I feel in my bones there is not much time to do waist. We need to act. Is there way to discern what to do now?"

Sage began to walk with Sarah, he glanced nervously at her, as if he wanted to say something, but thought better of it. She looked at him, narrowing her eyes, "You're hiding something from the twins, aren't you?"

Sage, wide-eyed shook his head, "No, not really. Marshall knows the truth. Ira won't admit it. He blames Albagoth, when it is his mom he needs to blame."

Sarah considered that. "I saw the events at the statue. I know you're Tomás. I don't understand why you changed your name or changed my name, for that matter."

"You're getting a head of yourself, Sarah. Sage is a title I was given once I finished my training with all the different spiritual teachers and mentors on many worlds. Those that know me personally prefer to call me Tomás. The twins used to. It's when Marshall began to call me "Father" that Ira stopped listening to me. You didn't see all the years I spent trying to counsel, guide and teach them. The statue was only supposed to show you key elements of their lives. There is so much more that can't be shared."

"I suppose so. What I don't understand is how am I going to convince these two paths to accept the Murdocs? They live peacefully and do not require them to change their belief pattern," Sarah said.

"You haven't been here long enough to for us to show you what all we follow," Albaohman Davineh butted in. "It isn't a belief we follow. It's a knowing."

"Maybe so," Sarah said softly. "I need time to let everything soak in. I've had a lot happen since I got here. Once we get to the town center, let's group together to see who is going with us and how we're going to plan to get Xander out."

They walked in silence. Thoughts swirled in Sarah's mind, replaying all she saw and heard. *Albagoth, not sure if you guide me or if I am supposed to come to my own conclusions. I've heard Xander say to look to you, but I'm confused. If I am supposed to find my own path, show me what is best. How can I reach the twins?*

The answer came is a soft voice within, that Ira is the only one she had to persuade. Once he knew beyond a doubt what is right, then his followers would adhere to what he said. Now that they believed he was who he said he was.

To Sarah, the voice and words sounded like something her intuition would say to her. *How do I know it you, Albagoth?*

Trust.

Trees rustled their leaves and a few birds began to sing. The song sounded reminded her of church bells mixed with the Asian drumming she'd seen in videos on YouTube. Her mom wanted to attend a touring Asian band concert that came to Boise a few years ago. She regretted they didn't go. She resolved to make sure they went the next time they came.

A twig snapped, jolting her out of her musing. Hearing Davineh say something, made her shake her head.

"What?" She looked at him, then noticed the birds were silent and the village had an eerie aura. Lynx and Manx padded softly to them.

"The birds were issuing a warning of what's to come," Davineh said. "We need to gather everyone together to listen to us." He turned to Sarah, "I know you still have questions and your training isn't complete. Your abilities to fight will come naturally. Though, we prefer peace and do not encourage weapons or killing others. We must find a way to free your friend and not risk you being lost in the battle of the paths."

Sarah nodded.

Milo and Geoffrey looked at each other and then Davineh and Sage.

"Did we miss something? I don't understand about the battle. I was told Sarah is the one who is in danger and needed to be protected," Milo said.

"I don't understand the what any of you are talking about. We landed in a beach area. And those trees opened up and swallowed Xander."

Davineh put his hands together, steepled his fingers, softly humming to himself. "It isn't easy to explain to you,

Milo. There's too much history to go over. Right now, we need to focus on the present."

They reached the center of the village. Davineh put his fingers to the corners of his mouth and blew, jolting the two teens, who reacted by inserting their fingers in their ears.

Other came rushing out of their dwellings.

"The birds send messages?" Milo whispered, a bit late.

'Maybe it's like Curá, Milo. Everything has consciousness. Every animal, avian, plant and humanoid know what's going on. They know what's going on. The birds wherever Xander is being held likely passed the message on."

"Oh."

"Kind of like that game we used to play as kids, Milo," Sarah added.

"What game?" Milo looked at her.

"Telephone. Only this time, the birds get the message right. With no changes to the original message."

"Okay . . ." Milo thought back, shook his head, "I don't remember that game. You must have played it after my transformation and the Tarradonnas took me to their world for schooling." Milo pouted. Deep down, he knew he missed a lot by not growing up as a human boy. His growth being interrupted by that accidental wish. "I wish I had experienced that."

"Hope you weren't touching your hands or thighs when you made that wish," Geoffrey muttered.

Everyone circled around Albaohman Davineh. He stood in the middle. "Sarah, come stand with me." Sarah felt all eyes on her as she walked to stand near him. "Everyone, Sarah is the Lost Princess. Most of you have met her. The prophecy is coming to fulfillment. Now is the time for us to act to protect our village as well as to help her. She hasn't finished her training and all her questions as to why we had to hide her have not been answered. We have a major problem at hand. Sarah brought with her three friends. One has been captured by the Wraiths and is being held to lure her in to rescue him. We need our best guards and spiritual vanguards to accompany her to get him. Who wants to go?"

Two of the guards that met Sarah and Lynx when they entered stepped forward. The females were taller than most of the Murdocs and carried staffs, as well as other tools that could be used for weapons.

"We will go, Albaohman Davineh. Albagoth has shown us how to protect her and how to be merciful to the Wraiths despite how horrible they have treated us."

"Very good, Marimeth and Salinom. You two are two of our best spiritual vanguards. Anyone else?"

Milo, Geoffrey and Lynx stepped forward, "We will go. We don't know your ways, but Xander is our friend. Sarah is, also."

"Very good. Any friend of Sarah's is a friend of ours. Sage? What about you?"

Sage glanced at Manx. Manx nodded. "Yes, we will go. I sense the Failed Saviors are there with the Wraiths. Someone needs to beseech Marshall to come to help us negotiate with his followers.

Sarah glanced around, amazed by all the people who agreed to follow her. Yet something tugged in her gut; something didn't feel right. She reflected on Xander being angry that she wouldn't allow him to help her when he realized she wasn't as weak as he assumed she was. And her wanting to fight her own battles. She didn't go to Curá or into the Shadowlands to usurp Xander's hero status. She went because she wanted a journey. Her life in Nampa was getting boring. She also wanted answers to her own questions. Why was she dreaming about spiders and the circles with the many divisions? She didn't find all the answers there. Once here in Wayla, she is finding her answers. There is still a large part of her that says she must do this herself. Taking a deep breath, letting it out slowly, her confusion ebbed away. With a clear mind, the answer comes to her she has to accept this help. There is so much about Wayla she doesn't know.

"I'm blown away by all the support you all have given me. Especially since you all don't know me. Yet you put your trust in me," Sarah said.

The crowd roars with laughter.

"What?" Sarah blurts out.

"You're a young woman in our ways, Princess Sarah. Though your Murdoc DNA is coming to the forefront, you aren't familiar with this territory. The twins changed the landscape after the Failed Savior died to his savior status. They created the maze to further confuse and prevent travelers from other worlds to find us Murdocs and so we couldn't find them. Yet we have the secret tunnels that help us find out way to their villages when needed," one of the guards stated.

"We volunteered because you know your magical abilities are not fully formed. We want peace as much as you do," said another woman who came forward.

"In assisting you to free your friend, we can distract the Wraiths and Fallen Saviors enough so you can speak with the Wraith in private. Once you get him alone, speak to his Murdoc self. The hurt human will melt away. You wound him with a stun word, he will collapse. We hope his spirit will go to Alabgoth where he can have a conversation with the genderless one," Davineh stated.

Milo, Geoffrey and Sarah glanced at each other, "Stun word?"

"I don't know how to do a stun word," Sarah said.

"You used your daydreams to make an atom bomb, but it was a mild compared to what your world has experienced. In this way, you use your imagination or daydream to stun Ira. The more upset, angry and convinced he has to destroy you, the easier it will be to influence him to pass out, and for his spirit to float out of his body," Davineh explained.

Chapter 13

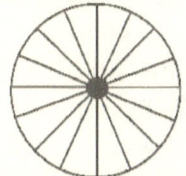

Ira paced back and forth outside the parameter of the village, fuming about his followers and the Failed Saviors taking over his kidnapping. Holding his scythe in a death grip, down lengthways, he muttered, trying to figure out how he would take back the control of the whole campaign.

"They have to listen to me! I'm their god! Or their demon. I'm the one who is the master mind here. How did this get so out of control?"

The air prickled, causing Ira's hair to poof out like puffer fish. He turned around several times, looking for someone, "Marshall? Marshall! Where are you? I know it's you!"

He felt someone tap him on the back. He turned around to see his brother standing there, waving his fingers on his right hand.

"Hellu," Marshall smiled, glowing all over.

"You got to be kidding! Have you gone to that strange world again with those guys that don't act like . . ."

"I don't know what you mean!" Marshall, smiled impishly, flipping a limp wrist to push the words away. He straightened up. "I will be serious. Ira, you and I have got to stop this. Let Xander go. He hasn't done anything."

"He's in this with the Murdoc Princess. I know he is. He dropped in this world at the same time, therefore he's helping her to bring back the throne and they will force us all to be Murdocs and follow their tree worship!" Ira fumed.

Marshall chuckled, shaking his head. "Brother, it isn't like that. Xander knows nothing about Sarah's calling. He only wants to protect her because she's a girl. He doesn't know about her ability to channel her innate to create protection through connecting with the trees, Wayla and nature in her imagination."

"Huh?" Ira wrinkled up his nose.

"How do you think we were able to make the changes to our world after we re-surfaced from the Black Hole? How were we able to create the realm we live in above Wayla, overseeing all that goes on?"

Ira shrugged, "We're gods, Marshall. Mom said we were part god because the nameless one is our father. I used that god power to do the amazing things and the special words that make me invisible . . ."

Marshall held up one finger, "But you can't use those special words to make your followers believe you are really the Wraith, correct?"

"Well . . . no – they think it is just a legend and they are worshipping some hidden demon that they won't ever see in entity." He thought about what Marshall said about Xander not seeing Sarah as powerful. "Women are more powerful than the men, here on Wayla. How can Xander not know that?"

"Xander comes from a world that sees their women as weak, though they underestimate them. They put more emphasis on a woman being pretty, thin and looking good for their men. Xander believes those myths. So at as a teen, he believes he has to protect her. His world frowns on women fighting, working and taking care of themselves. Equality is a foreign concept to them."

"How do you know?" Ira dropped his scythe, skeptical of what his brother said.

"Our birth father took me to that world while I was exploring the Black Hole you made. I was gone for six months."

"Birth father? You met the Nameless One?" Ira's eyes grew to the size of plates.

Marshall laughed, "No, Tomás. Tomás is our real father, Ira. He taught us so much and there was so much you refused to admit or even sit and listen to."

Ira was lost for words, he stood there, just blinking.

"Mother tried to tell you and you accused her of lying. Open your eyes and your heart."

Ira narrowed his eyes, turned away. *I can't lower myself to believe this. I'm special, that's why I can do the things I do.*

"We're both half-human and half-Murdoc, Ira. That's why we can do what we do. Forgive Mother. Forgive the genderless Creator of All Worlds and Forgive others you think wronged you."

"No! I refuse to forgive anyone! Most of all myself! I didn't do anything wrong! You're living a lie, Marshall! You know Tomás can't be our father! You know the Murdocs are evil! After all, they kicked mother out of the village and made her give up the throne! We have a right to that throne – not that lost princess! We and our descendants are the ones who should take that place."

Marshall tutted. Sighing, "Brother, can you name any of your children or great-great-grandchildren?"

"Maybe."

Marshall explained, "I can't because we weren't allowed to claim in public we had spouses and produced children. If anyone knew about my wife, she would have been put to death, too. I wouldn't be able to save her unless she revealed her Murdoc abilities. Or I revealed mine. Didn't you have the same problem?"

Ira turned back around, his head lowered, he slowly lifted his face to show the defeated expression. He remembered his love, River and how she used to sing to him. They spent so many days by the beach, running, chasing each other and the love he felt with each baby they brought into the world. But she didn't want to be a Wraith follower. She was from the Village and loved her Murdoc parents and neighbors. She also loved her Anansi and wouldn't go many places without her close by. She also had a close relationship with a tree she often meditated with. It broke his heart to find out she preferred to raise their children in the Murdoc way.

"I couldn't go public with River. She loved her family more than me and couldn't understand the movement I was undertaking." Ira looked up to his brother, his face crumbled and heartbreak showing through his eyes. Ira fought back the tears, looking away quickly as tears began to fall. He brought up his left arm and wiped them away with the sleeve of his black robe. After a deep intake of breath he let it in one large sigh, clearing his throat and gaining his control once again. He again turned toward his brother.

"We can't be Murdoc, Marshall. Mother said we're full gods."

"Mother was a Murdoc Princess, brother. That means we are part Murdoc. We both tried to deny it. My etching appeared when I was 15. Yours never did. A friend and I discovered a way to get it to fade, though. My offspring also learned to suppress theirs and taught it to their friends who remained in the Failed Savior Village."

Marshall stepped forward, "Deep down you know we can't fight Sarah. She isn't as lost and helpless as you believe her to be. She's a strong Murdoc Woman. In addition, she was raised with humans, who have imparted in her the importance of being an individual. Now that she's home, she will use the Murdoc instincts that are coming out to figure a way to get each path working together. She won't ask us to abandon our belief systems."

"How do you know? According to the prophecy you uttered, she would," Ira spat, his dark eyes turning to stone.

"Over the centuries, my words have been twisted. That isn't what I was shown before I fell off the tree and you pulled me all the way down. I was shown she would find a way to get us to accept each other. Yes, she is younger than I saw in the vision, but this is according to what Albagoth intended."

"Don't say that name! You know as well as I that entity refuses to acknowledge us! We are his sons!" Ira shook a fist at him.

"Calm, brother. Albagoth is genderless. I spent some time with the genderless one after we parted ways. I was supposed to be dead, remember? And you thought I did pass. My spirit rose above, and I met the genderless one in the space beyond space. The bigger picture is the Creative Spirit resides in all of us. In all Murdocs, you, me, humans, Anansi and much more. It's how we chose to live our lives that matter. Learning to accept each other as they are and not seeking to change them."

Ira shook his head. "I don't believe you, Marshall. You've always been the one to look on the bright side of life. You never see the dark side. Mother tried to get you to live in balance. There must be something bad. Seeing the bad is healthy. Watching the Murdocs be destroyed is the greatest aspiration I can have. My followers understand…only…"

"Only they don't want to follow you. They don't believe you are the real Wraith. They see the Wraith as a spirit or symbol that they aspire to become, correct?"

"Yes. I want to lead them in their march into the Murdocs to create the havoc I inspired them to do, but they won't accept my role." Ira looked at his brother, "What about your followers? Have you tried to reach out to them?"

"Oh, yes, of course. But they don't believe I'm who I say I am. Especially because I've come clean. I'm letting them know they have misunderstood my teachings. They won't listen to me. They have to make their own way."

Ira sighed, wiped his forehead and yawned. "I'm tired and I have a stress headache coming on. I wish I knew what to do. Maybe I could firebomb my followers in the hopes they'd listen to me."

Marshall chuckled. Walking up to him, he lightly slapped him on the back, "Let's go back to the Murdoc village and get some food. I heard you gave Xander Veh up to your followers in the hopes of capturing Sarah?"

"Yeah, and that's how it started to go all wrong. I made a huge mistake to lure him away from that griffin and his friend. Now I fear Xander's life is in real danger and I feel helpless."

"We can change that, Ira," Marshall smiled.

"How?"

"We have our Murdoc tricks that our followers don't believe in. Also Sarah and her new family are on their way to rescue Xander. We can insure they get him out safely."

"Okay." He replayed what his brother just said. "Wait. Sarah's whole family are coming to rescue him? Sarah's supposed to come alone."

"You underestimate the unity that resides within the Murdoc village and Sarah's friends. Trust, brother."

Chapter 14

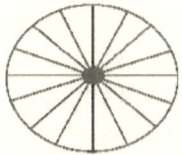

Sarah lead the procession still not sure how they would free Xander. She didn't know what to expect. Lynx, getting good at balancing on his hindlegs, came up, followed by Milo and Geoffrey.

"We're a team," Milo, Lynx and Geoffrey said together. "We won't leave you all alone."

Glancing at them, she flashed a weak smile, "I know that, fellows." She looked back forward, wishing she had more time with her tree friend. Nickoli wasn't too far behind them.

"You're worried about something," Milo piped up. "I wouldn't be close friend if I didn't ask what it is."

Sarah lifted a shoulder and the opposite hand to brush it away. "It's nothing. I can't pinpoint what it is that bothers me, Milo. I just got to find Xander. I know he wants to protect me. He's upset that he wasn't the one to open to Shadowlands and that I can protect myself. Yet right now, he's the one that must be rescued. As usual, I'm the one fighting his battles. For all his ability to see through another person, he trusts the wrong person. I have a feeling that Wraith character tried to charm him and lead him to believe nothing bad would happen to him. I'm supposed to unite three paths or just find a way for them to realize neither has to change their spiritual practices, but accept each other without killing the path they're the most afraid of. Or killing each other."

"You don't know how to do that, do you?" Milo asked.

"That about sums it up. I mean, how many 15-year-old females would be faced with something like this? I'm not Wonder Woman," Sarah glanced at her friend.

Milo put his palms together and started rubbing them to heat up his wish gift, "Would you like to be?"

Sarah laughed. "I know you could give it to me instantly, but that would be cheating, my friend. My Anansi, the Sage of Stillness and the Banyan trees I've meet said I have to find the answers myself by looking within myself."

Milo nodded, "Yes, that water goddess told me the same thing. But there are also comes a time to look beyond the situation to see another way to solve the issue. Sometimes we get too close to the problem that we can't see the meadow through the trees."

Sarah felt a heavy weight lifted off her shoulders.

"You have a good point." She looked at him, "Thank you. I hadn't thought of that."

Nickoli dropped down from a tree branch on a thin silk thread, landing on Sarah's left.

"Don't worry, Sarah, we all are with you. We will all have a part in guiding you," he reminded her. Sarah gave him a weak smile and nodded at the same time. Even though she knew they all were with her, there was a nagging dread that something wasn't going the way they meant it to. She admitted they didn't have a plan. Just a weak, "Let's wing it here."

Please, Albagoth, guide me or us in what to do.

"What could go wrong?" Lynx chimed in. "I have thumbs, they will be handy. And I have mastered walking on my hind legs."

"Don't be smug, Lynx," Geoffrey bumped him with his shoulder.

"Smug? Me?" Lynx grinned. Those that knew him well, laughed.

Xander woke with a massive headache and with the right side of his face hurting as if he fell on it. His arms, wrapped behind a tree and tightly bound to it, and ached. He struggled to find a way to loosen the ropes. Glancing around him, he wondered where the group was that had surrounded him hours ago. He took a deep breath and let it out, wondering what would happen to him. He trusted that Wraith character. He planned on double crossing him, only to be double crossed instead.

"I'm not very smart," he sighed. "Now Sarah is walking in a trap if she chooses to come free me. Or maybe she will let me rot here because I was so nasty and resentful of her being better than me. I wish I had the kind of magic or whatever she had to bond with a tree. I wonder if I need to be a Murdoc to talk with a tree."

A Fallen Savior follower, dressed in a yellow robe instead of orange, approached him, taking his hood down, he revealed his engraving of a boulder blocking one path and another opening on the other side of it. He held a staff with a craved circle with many divisions. He lifted it and muttered some words Xander couldn't hear.

"I wasn't here," the boy said, then he uttered another set of words and disappeared.

Xander wasn't sure what that was about. Gradually his back began get warm. Next, he felt the tree expanding and the ropes snapped as the tree also grew taller and wider. Next, he fell backward. As he fell, Xander noticed a golden sparkling light all around him. The tree sealed itself, shrunk to its normal size and the ropes drifted up and reunited together.

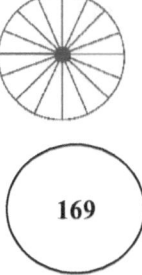

A Fallen Savior follower, dressed in a yellow robe approached Sarah's Murdoc group. Sarah eyes grew wide, recognizing him. She glanced behind her, "Lynx, come forward next me. We have trouble."

Lynx ran forward, using his staff to help with his balance, stopping when he reached her side.

"Halt. Everyone, just stop right here," Sarah commanded, holding up a hand. The group obeyed but crowded around to find out what was happening.

When the young boy reached Sarah, he took down his hood to reveal the same engraving Lynx took on when he shapeshifted into the kid to rescue Sarah.

"Hello, Princess. I'm Darrel. I was planning on freeing you when that furry creature there," he pointed to Lynx, "attacked him and I watched him shift into my doppelganger. He's a menace and an evil one. Look, he still holds my favorite staff."

"Lynx, what do you have to say for yourself?" Sarah asserted.

Lynx held up his paws, dropping the staff. "I'm sorry, I didn't get your name or ask your permission. I just knew you were sympatric to my plight but didn't stop to think you were planning the same thing I was. I needed to pass off as Fallen Savior to get close to Sarah, my friend." Lynx bent down, picked up the staff, "Here, you can have this back. I'm sorry, I didn't mean to attack you or hurt you. I hope your head doesn't hurt too badly where I conked you over the head with your staff."

"You did what?" Sarah roared. "You said he was asleep. You didn't tell me you clobbered him."

Lynx shrunk down a bit. "Well, I had to put him to sleep so he wouldn't tell anyone I borrowed his shape."

Sarah let out a frustrated hiss, "Lynx, if I ever find out you hurt someone again just to shape into that person – I – Jupiter Crying out loud cities!"

"You don't have to cuss," Milo eased.

Collectively the Murdocs asked, "What's a Jupiter?"

Another lone voice asked, "Are their cities nice? Large with bright lights?"

Everyone began talking at once, each saying wondering, or admonishing Lynx or speculating on what a Jupiter was.

"Grrrr!" Sarah growled, not knowing how to address their concerns. Besides, Jupiter wasn't even the issue.

Sage moved forward, turned around facing the crowd and Sarah, held up his hands to quiet the murmuring.

"Everyone, settle down. Let Princess Sarah calm down." He looked at Lynx, "You and I will have a talk later about this. Right now isn't a good time." Turning to Darrel, "I see you are leaving the Fallen Saviors before you get found out you're a heretic. Does this mean you will help us free the other Indigo Traveler named Xander?"

"Yes, I will. I will also help you unite the three paths. I'm not sure what your plans are. I only know what Albagoth has been showing me in my dreams. But I warn you, the tree Xander has been tied to has swallowed him."

"Swallowed him?" Sarah, Milo and Geoffrey said in unison.

"We will see to that when we get there," Sage took charge. "Darrel, lead us. Pick up your other staff and let's go."

"Whoa, how does he know the tree swallowed Xander?" Sarah asked, not believing what she heard.

"And why would a tree do something like that?" Milo added.

"And why would they tie him to a tree?" Geoffrey added.

"Those questions don't matter right now," Sage answered. "Darrel, lead us. I'll walk with you."

Darrel nodded his consent to leading. Bending down to pick it up, he grinned inward, revealed they accepted him.

He released his worries, grabbed the spare staff, stood up, and turned to Lynx, "Here, I have another. You can keep this because you need it to help you balance. I see you're still shaky on your back legs."

Lynx accepted it, though he was amazed at the generosity.

"Thank you, Darrel. I'm sorry. I'm also sorry I didn't find out your name before I left. I had to hurry to rescue Sarah."

Darrel nodded. Sage patted the young teen on the shoulder to get his attention. He looked at the tall Sage.

"Remove your robe. I hope you have on your tunic and leggings under that."

"Yes, sir, I do." Darrel removed his robe and tossed it on the side of the road. "I know a quick way to get to my former village. We need to hurry because the Wraiths and my people are planning to raid your village tonight. Xander is safe, though. We just have to insure Sarah is safe, as well."

"No, we need Sarah with us when we begin negotiations with two spiritual paths. Have you seen the Wraith?" Sage replied, waving for others to follow him and Darrel with a wave of his left hand.

"I saw a man dressed in an all-black robe, like the Wraith followers. He carried a curved tool like the statues of the Wraith. He claimed to be the legendary Wraith, but he followers refused to accept him. Their leader pushed him aside and took charge of the group. The Wraith was the one that brought Xander to them. Marshall accompanied my village to the Wraith's village. And then disappeared, saying he had to find his brother." Darrel walked quickly, trying to keep up with the Sage of Stillness. "Their brothers, aren't they? The Wraith and the Fallen Savior?"

"Yes, they are twins. And my kin," Sage admitted.

"How can they still be alive after all these years? And the Fallen Savior was supposed to have died once he landed in the Black Hole," Darrel observed.

Sage opened his mouth to say something, and then closed it, considering what to say. Manx came up to his other side.

"Can you explain how you're still alive, too? After all, you've been around much longer than the twins," Manx prodded him.

"Point taken, my friend. That is hard to explain, but I can after this all over," he answered Manx. "Darrel, the answer to your question will have to wait until we've settled this matter."

"I can wait," the teen agreed.

Xander walked down a hallway lite by long tubes giving the tunnel a soft, golden glow. Though, the light also sparkled, as if everything had been dusted with fairy dust. The tunnel itself looked like it was made from brass, or metal of some kind. He noticed other types of light fixtures hanging from the ceiling down side tunnels from chains. Somewhere in there, a ceiling fan echoed through the passages, whirling away.

Xander's heart pounded. His hairs all over his body stood on end. His thoughts spun in circles, *where am I? And why would that kid want me to be inside this tree? Will I ever get out of here? And see Sarah, Milo, Geoffrey and my parents again? Oh my spirit! How I've hurt Sarah! I truly am the weak one. She always has to save me. When I can ever be strong enough to save myself?*

"My child, strength doesn't show itself in coming forward to fight off those who would harm your loved ones. Though, that is one way. Strength comes from admitting you're wrong and finding another way to help them."

Xander stopped in open, "Who speaks to me?"

A noise echoed through the chambers, sounding like a person was dragging its feet. Xander thought of Cranny, back at Curá, and how his roots would sound if he was in this tunnel. Xander smiled, hoping to see that wonderful Criata. Instead, a tall, slender tree, with long weeping branches came into view.

"Hello, my Indigo Traveler. I'm the one you were strapped to. It was my shell they tied you to. My true self stands before you. I'm Noble. Darrel, the Fallen Savior teen who opened up this passage, answered my call as I broadcast your desire to speak to me the way the Princess Sarah speaks to my relatives, the Banyan trees."

"Broadcast? That's creepy. In my world, we would call you all insane for broadcasting out thoughts like that," Xander replied. He felt tiny bugs crawling up and down his skin and back. Brushing them off nervously, he wondered what it was. Looking down, he noticed tiny spiders. "Eeep!"

Noble's leaves and branches rustled like a spring wind building intensity. Xander wondered what was happening, until he realized the tree was laughing at him.

"What's so funny about spiders crawling on me?"

Noble calmed himself, taking a deep breath, "My dear young man, those are not spiders. Those are baby Anansis. They are welcoming to our world and long to become friends and guides to you. They will grow up enough to go live above ground with the Murdocs and be paired with a young Murdoc to finish their training together."

The Anansis continued climbing on Xander, some on his bare skin on his arms and neck. "Hey, that tickles," he said, wiggling, bending his head to one side and twisting his body away from them.

"Little Ones, you're distracting us from our exploration," Noble said, clapping two branches together, "time to climb off and go find your nurse maid,"

"Yes, Noble," little voices chimed. They ran down Xander, though a few spun quick silk threads and flew off, giggling and urging others to come chase them.

"They're just like children," Xander watched wide eyed.

"Come follow me. As we walk, you can share with me why you wished to speak to us," Noble guided.

Words left Xander. "I –um I- um," he reflected to his thoughts and frustrations. "I wanted to be like my friend, Sarah, who spoke to a tree last week when we were in Curá. We were trapped in the Shadowlands and she found a tree and it told her how to unlock the Shadowlands so the Crow Judges could come in. I just thought if I could speak to the tree I was bound to, I could find out why the Wraiths bound me to it and maybe I could figure out a way to solve the anguish the Wraiths and Fallen Saviors are having. Maybe the Murdocs need their own land so they will leave the two alone and stop asking them to change."

Noble stopped in his tracks. "What makes you think the Murdocs are the one to causing the trouble?"

"Well, it—er-um," Xander's face grew hot as he realized he misspoke, but he couldn't back down. "It's just normally the person or group that others are fighting against that is usually in the wrong, right?" *Oh, Albagoth, I sure am in deep doo now. How can I get myself out this?*

"First off, Xander, Sarah has a way with trees, being her Murdoc DNA is coming through the human DNA mask is fading away. By the time you all go back to your home world, Sarah will be showing more of her Murdoc traits. You are 100 per cent human . . ."

"Then how come we are talking?" Xander jutted his chin out.

Noble's appearance grew stern, his once relaxed and flexible branches and leaves became stiff, his voice steady, but taunt, "We are talking because Albagoth inspired it. You made a desire known we found a way to answer it. You would grow in wisdom to listen without challenging me or threatening the Murdocs."

"I'm not threatening them! I was held captive. I don't know much about this world or these people. I'm completely lost here. I thought I was lost back home, but here it much worse. And those mazes . . ."

"Will be sorted out after the lost princess decides what to do," Noble interrupted. "Are you ready to learn, Master Xander?"

"I don't know," he stared at the ground. "I'm not much for following rules are spitting out what the teachers say in my classes." His stomach dropped, as he realized school would be starting soon and his mom was likely worried about them getting home.

"The lessons you are learning don't relate to what your society and community want you to know, Xander. The lessons are spiritual and will help you with your physical plane as well as your emotional, mental and interpersonal relationships. They will also help you relate to yourself. Are you ready?" Noble relaxed a bit.

"I suppose so. But you had one thing to lecture me about. The Murdocs and the other two villages. I don't understand what the whole fight is about."

Noble lifted the two branches on each side of his trunk, which Xander interpreted as a smile. "I was getting to that, child." The tree appeared to be reflecting on its words. "You're not a child. You're a young man. With a lot of growing and maturing to do. Come, let us continue our walk. Once we get to where we are going, you will see and understand much more. Forgiveness is the key to so much."

Xander wondered what forgiveness had to do with it. After all, he still felt like he had to be the hero. The one to save the day. Sarah has stolen his thunder. Aren't men supposed to be stronger, braver and more able to protect the women? Who has ever heard of a woman protecting a man?"

Noble smacked a branch against the wall, picked up his left group of roots and smacked it down hard. The abrupt smacks jarred Xander and echoed throughout the chamber. Xander's last words reverberated in his mind. He set his jaw, wishing for an answer, tensing up all his muscles resenting being ignored like a common child who didn't know enough to get in out of the rain.

Noble turned left at a fork in the passage way. Xander started to keep going straight. Xander stopped when he realized Noble wasn't in front of him. He turned around and headed back to the fork, looked down to the right and the fading image of the tree.

 Noble stopped in the large room with a fire place burning some of kind of element that wasn't wood and large bean bag shaped like a mushroom group.

"Have a sat. I know you're hungry and thirsty. Food is coming," Noble said. He dragged his roots over to a small pool and lifted his roots one at a time to get in. "Aah, that feels good. I can't go too long without drinking, either."

A small humanoid came in with a tray of sandwiches made of out of course grain, with lettuce, cheese and some kind of meat. And a tall glass of water. Xander took it, thanked the person and took a large drink and then a bite of the sandwich. As he chewed, he hoped his friends were getting enough food, too.

"You have questions. I can't guarantee I have all the answers. My specialty is guiding the individual to find their truth by looking within. What is your first question, my son?"

177

Xander swallowed a large bite. Cleared his throat softly, relaxed as he considered. "What is my role here in this world? What is my role back home? And how can I help Sarah if I'm not supposed to fight for her?"

Noble raised his branches closest to his trunk, bending his top branches up and down like a nod. "You are showing you've been considering what to say as we walked in silence. Now, close your eyes, consider each question one at a time and listen to that small voice within you answer."

"What about…"

"No, Xander. Don't ask me. Ask your inner self. That is the part of you that is Albagoth left there for you."

Xander closed his eyes, took a deep a breath and let it out slowly, recalling his mom leading him in how to center, and focus.

Chapter 15

Marshall studied the tree with the hemp ropes around it. He reached over and tugged at the ropes, hoping there would be some clue as to why the ropes were there. He shook his head and sighed. Then he remembered his followers and the Wraiths tied up Xander. He touched the trunk, wondering where Xander disappeared to. It felt warm. He studied the ground near the tree, remembering the Black Hole Ira dug for him to fall through. He heard the Sage and a group of Murdocs approaching from behind. Ira entered came up to him dressed in some black tunic and trousers carrying his scythe.

"Okay, Marshall, I'm leaving my Wraith image behind me. But I still want to torment all Murdocs and punish them for hurting Mother," Ira pouted.

When his brother didn't respond, he noticed his brother was upset. "What's wrong?"

"Xander is missing. What did our followers do with him? And is he all right?" Marshall asked.

Ira leaned his head to one side, considering his brother's concern. "You really care about this human. Why? We don't know him from anyone and he isn't from Wayla."

"He is one of Albagoth's creations. He has a soul like us, Ira. We must look after each other. Don't you understand?" Marshall roared.

Ira backed up a few paces. His twin's anger and anguish took him off guard. He didn't know what to say.

The Murdoc group reached them. They stopped and stood around the tree.

"Marshal, Ira," Sage greeted his sons. "I didn't expect to see you here."

"Hello, Sage Tomás," Ira replied. "I didn't expect to see you here."

"Greetings, Sage Tomás," Marshall turned to embrace him. He looked over the group, "Greetings to you, my friends…travelers from the Worlds of Nampa and Curá. You have come not to crucify me again, right?"

The Murdocs laughed.

"They weren't the ones that crucified you, Marshall," Darrel spoke up. "My people were. Your very followers who were angered you understood the Murdocs. And understood we are all one. I understand that, too. I would like an Anansi."

"That isn't the time or place to discuss that, Darrel," Sage turned to him. Darrel lowered his head. "Marshall, something bothers you."

"Xander Veh, the other traveler from the World of Nampa was tied to this tree. This is the very tree my followers, as Darrel mentioned, tied me to eons ago. And the hole that the Wraith dug for me to fall into has been sealed, but marked with this stone, though, small. It is here."

Marshall looked somber, "Where did he go? And is he safe? Or has he been injured? What is more troubling, is that these ropes have been broken. Look."

Darrel smiled, basked in the work he did. His incantation worked wonderfully.

Xander walked strolled out from the left side of the group, looking refreshed and well-fed. Glancing at the group, he felt loss of words to say.

"What's going on? Why is everyone standing around Noble?"

"What?" the whole group exclaimed at once.

"Noble," Xander walked over to the tree and patted it. "This is Noble's dwelling." As he patted it, the ropes broke. Once they hit the soil, they turned to dust.

Sarah ran to him, "You're okay!" she hugged him without thinking.

Xander stiffened, then relaxed. "Yeah, I'm okay. But we must worry about what to do next. I mean, you have community to deal with."

"We?" Sarah let go and looked at him.

"You aren't doing this alone, Sarah." Xander waved at all the people gathered around behind them. Sarah turned. "These people and I will help you. You are never alone in this."

She nodded, glancing at him, she noticed he did have a few bruises on his face. She reached up and touched them lightly, sending a tingle throughout her body, "What happened?"

"The Wraiths and the Fallen Saviors took turns slapping me for screaming and yelling. That wasn't very manly of me, I guess. I didn't know how to protect myself or behave. I have a better idea of what to do, now. I want to thank the brave Fallen Savior boy for helping me." He looked out at the crowd and saw Darrel.

"I'm sorry I wasn't there for you," Sarah whispered. "I should have been."

"No, it isn't your fault. We each have our paths to follow, Sarah. I'm sorry for acting like a spoiled brat. Let's put that behind us now and look at this world. We have to see how we can help and guide them."

Sarah nodded in response. Hearing the crowd sigh, reminded them they weren't alone. They broke apart, blushing.

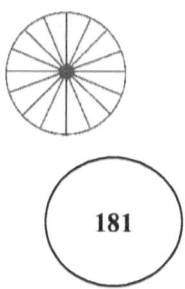

A hush fell over the group, Sarah and Xander self-consciously walked back to the group. Everyone began to nervously look around themselves, aware that something wasn't right. Xander remembered the trap.

"I was here to trap you. Once you came, the Wraiths and the Fallen Saviors were supposed to capture you," Xander said.

Ira shook his head, "That is what I wanted to happen. They kicked me out and made their own plan. It's too quiet here. I suggest we split up into groups and search the place looking for others. I suggest the Murdoc soldier surround Sarah and protect her."

Sarah' mouth dropped, "You're the Wraith! And you want the Murdoc's guard protecting me? What changed?"

"I haven't changed my fear of you, Princess. I only am fighting to get control of my people back. They don't recognize me as the living Wraith. So I appear as I am. Ira son of Miriam. The Princess that was ex-communicated from the Murdoc village."

"Whoa, if you…" Xander started to say something Manx and the Sage spoke up.

"Later, Xander."

"Do what my son says," Sage answered.

"I'm not your son! I'm the son of the Nameless One," Ira barked.

"Give it a rest, Ira!" Marshall rolled his eyes. He walked away from Ira and joined Sarah, the Sage, Manx, Lynx and Nickoli.

Each group paired off and the Sage divided up the village.

Milo, Geoffrey and Xander went one way. Darrell glanced around, not knowing who to join. He decided to join Milo and Xander. He ran to catch up, "May I join you all?"

"Sure," Milo said.

"I've never seen a life Griffin before," Darrell said. "The Sage used to tell us stories about Griffins from your world and how brave they are. But we always thought it was myths. My people said all the Sage's stories were myths with no truth in them," Darrel went on.

Xander gritted his teeth. Milo smiled.

"All myths have some grain of truth," Milo answered. "In our world, myths and legends are used to teach us some characteristic or attribute we need to take in ourselves. All stories have some lessons in them. Some are hidden in the entertainment and others are there straight forward."

"Hogwash! Milo, you're are leading the poor boy on," Xander admonished. "Darrel, you need to make up your own mind. Don't listen to metal brain here. He makes up his own stories, you know."

"You do?" Darrel said in awe.

"I'm a writer. I'm also have the gift of granting wishes," Milo explained. They heard a noise to their left.

"So you be careful what you wish for while touching him," Geoffrey added. "We better turn left here to see what the noise is."

"I'll go," Mil volunteered.

"No, we stick together," Xander reminded them.

"This place is eerie. No one is here." Darrel drew out each word, speaking as softly as he could.

A flash of green, stiff bristles burst out from the left side, at the first opening of the alley way. It snatched Milo and disappeared as quickly as it could.

The others stood still, not knowing what to do.

"Now what?" Geoffrey asked. "We can't follow."

"I haven't seen pine trees here," Xander added.

"What are pine trees?" Darrel asked.

"Noble firs are on your world, Xander," Geoffrey replied.

"I didn't say it was a Noble fir. The only Noble I met wasn't a fir tree. He called himself a Wisdom tree."

"Do trees have genders?" Geoffrey asked.

"Come on, let's find the Sage. He'll know what to do," Darrel went off to the right. The other two followed him.

Sage of Stillness, Marshall and Sarah stood in the middle of the village glancing around. Nickoli rose up on his back legs, as if he was sniffing the air. Manx did the same thing, pulling his lips up to get a better scent. Lynx ran a paw through his whiskers and fur on his head, and then shook himself.

Sarah glanced at them, "What's wrong, Nickoli? You sense something."

"Something isn't right, Sarah. Someone should be here. The trap isn't here, that's for sure," Sage replied, putting one hand on his hip, holding his staff with the other.

"Our village is in danger," Nickoli exclaimed. We need to get back there.

Sage, sensing the frantic emotions rising in his group, put his staff in the crook of his elbow, placed his out, palms downward, "Let's all breathe deep and let it out slowly." They each did so about three times. "Now, join hands with me, and the person closest to me, touch me. I have a vortex space manipulator. I'll set it our village and we'll go."

"What about the others in the group?" Sarah asking, putting her hand inside the Sage's elbow.

"Sage! Sage! Milo disappeared! Something green snatched him!" Darrel yelled.

The other groups surrounded them.

"We can't worry about that, now. We must get back to the Murdoc village. The Wraiths and Fallen Saviors are there."

"How do you know?" Someone in Albaohman Davineh's group asked.

"Just a feeling Nickoli and Manx have," Sage said. "We trust our inner voice. Come on, everyone, join hands and the person on my left touch me. This is the quickest way to insure we get to the Murdoc village and don't end up somewhere else."

They all obeyed, agreeing.

Razbuator, the leader of the Wraiths stormed through the Murdoc village. He had a death grip on his staff, which had a curved half circle, "Search everywhere!" he ordered. "She has to be here. Round all those miserable little Murdocs up and bring them to the center of their meeting place. Round up their creepy Anansis, too. If any try to escape, incinerate them!"

His followers scurried around, breaking down doors into the dwellings, smashing pottery and cutting down anything that looked like it was used in worship or meditation.

"They aren't here!" Someone from the Fallen Saviors called.

One of the Murdoc caregivers of the little ones was roughly brought out, his hands tied behind him with a Fallen Savior on one side and a Wraith on the others.

"They aren't here! Sarah and our guardian went to your village, Razbuator, to free Xander!"

"You lie! The Lost Princess is supposed to be smarter than that. She would have known it was a trap and would have stayed here. After we kill her, then we will go back and kill that consort of hers!" Razbuator sneered. He approached the caregiver, thrusting his staff, catching the small man under his chin, "What are you? One of the wimpy caregivers?"

"I care for the babies. I'm one of them. We aren't wimpy. Our women are the warriors as well as a few chosen men. We divide up the responsibilities equally. Not all women are cut out to care for the children and not all men are cut out to be warriors."

Another set of Wraith and Fallen Savior followers came out with another Murdoc caregiver who was covered in flour and dirt. His face had bruises and cuts from being knocked around.

"This one won't talk," the Wraith follower said, pushing the little man to the ground. "She isn't here. I heard what the other one said. I believe him. After all, that guy who claimed to our god, the Wraith we worshipped, said the Lost Princess would go to the ends of Wayla to free that freak we tied up."

"He'll be swallowed by the tree!" shouted another Murdoc as he was brought out, by a third pair.

"You lie! Trees only swallow Murdocs! And that's only in your dreams! Trees are stupid objects with no wisdom or use except for wood to keep us warm and cook our food." Razbuator spat.

Razbuator removed his staff from the first man. He scowled at those who were in front of them.

"Burn the dwellings down! Find the Anansis and kill them all! We want to show their freaks who is in charge! We won't allow anyone to make use bow down to their false god!"

"Albagoth is not a god. The genderless one is the Creator of all Worlds and doesn't demand we worship or acknowledge it," said one of the caregivers.

"Albagoth leads us all to find our own path through going within us," said another.

Another added, "All paths are equal."

Others chimed in, "So it is."

As more Murdocs were brought out, Razbuator noticed that not all of them were caregivers. There were Albaohman among the captured. Their Anansis came out of hiding. One by one, the followers of each sect beheaded the

Anansis, except of Gretchen, Terrance's Anansi. And the Anansis that were Sarah and the Murdocs who were traveling back.

"Besides that phony guy who claimed to be our Wraith god was alive and well. We all know that the real Wraith lives in the Black Hole and won't ever surface except to punish the Murdocs for sending his mother away for her having a child that was part god."

"Don't you mean twins? Remember, the Wraith had a twin brother, our Fallen Savior," said a Fallen Savior follower.

"Who was weak! He believed in the goodness of these miserable good for nothing Murdocs! He couldn't even get them to convert to his way. Look at us! We have had more Murdocs come to our side than not. Those who found out that the trees don't talk to them and those who found their Anansi misguided them away from what they wanted. They joined us! How many converts can you all attest to?" Razbuator dared.

The Fallen Savior sputtered.

Sage and the Murdoc group materialized on the outskirts of the village. They heard the screams of the Murdocs who were still alive and were being tortured.

"Dear Albagoth, guide us," the whole group beseeched.

"Be careful as we approach," Albaohman walked to the front. "I fear what we may find."

"I agree," Sarah said. "Father," Sarah turned to Davineh, "We haven't had time to discuss what happened and why I was taken to the World of Nampa. I think I understand, though," she sputtered. "I know this isn't the time to say it. I saw it in a vision. I don't understand. But know somehow I am related to Ira and Marshall."

"That's true, Princess," Davineh answered. "Now isn't the time to talk about it. Come. The action required will come to you."

Xander and Sarah felt self-conscious, realizing they were still holding hands in front of everyone. Their faces both flushed as they broke apart.

"Okay, so what do we do now?" Sarah asked, walking back to the Sage. Xander followed her.

"We search the town for anyone who has been left. It's odd that the Wraiths weren't guarding this tree," Sage said.

"They weren't concerned about that. They assumed Xander wouldn't escape and believed no one would come to free him or fight to free him," Darrel spoke up. "My people disagreed, but Razbuator wouldn't listen to them. He threatened to kill anyone who spoke against him or disagreed."

Sage, Marshall and Davineh exchanged looks, each appeared to be communicating with each other. They nodded their consent.

The little Albaohman spoke up, "What did they decide?"

"They decided to raid the Murdoc village. They believed that the lost princess would be hiding out there. Razbuator believed she didn't love or care about Xander at all. He believed she would be looking out for herself. Because that is what he would do," Darrel answered. "He made everyone go with him. Even my former village."

"How did you escape?" Sage asked.

"The children weren't included in the raid. We were left in a room a room with nursemaids from both the Wraiths and my village. They didn't count on me being able to sneak away. They were all had us studying up on the stories of our spiritual training. I've learned ways to make myself invisible, so I snuck out."

Marshall stared at Ira. Ira flashed an innocent smile at him and looked away again. But continued to feel his brother's stern look boring a hole in the side of his face.

"What? I didn't teach him. Besides, he's your follower!" Ira retorted.

Marshall chuckled, shaking his head.

"No, I'm not Marshall's follower. Just because I was raised as a Fallen Savior, doesn't mean I remain. I'm converting to the Murdocs. They have the right idea. All paths are equal. We are all one people. Albagoth spoke to me many times and I've befriended a young Anansis, too. I learned the invisibility incantation while meditating with a tree when I was nine," Darrel explained.

Lynx smiled.

"Why is that cat smiling?" Ira fumed.

"I'm not a cat. I'm a Werecat. A shapeshifter. I was drawn to Darrel because I sensed his decision to follow the Murdocs. I used his persona to free Sarah a day ago. I'm smiling because I chose well. But we're digressing. We need to go to the Murdoc Village. Your young and their caregivers are in danger. Sarah, what are you going to do?" Lynx said.

Sarah lowered her head, feeling despondent. "I don't feel qualified to help out. I still don't know what to do. Our people are being slaughtered because of me. How am I going to unite you all as one people?"

"We don't know for they are being slaughtered," Sage smiled. He took off his necklace with the unity symbol on it and put it around Sarah's neck.

"Princess Sarah, you are not uniting the people as one race of people. You show each one that it is okay to worship as they want while accepting the Murdocs for who they are. Besides, both the Fallen Saviors and the Wraiths are not all full blooded Murdocs. Some of them have the human blood that their twins have. Their children and their

189

children's children have left the Murdocs to join with the groups their fathers started," the Sage explained.

Sarah picked up the symbol around her neck, remembering parts of the prayer the Sage said when she, Petra and his Anansi were in that cage. "All paths lead to Albagoth," she uttered. Her thoughts spinning. "Albagoth leads each to within. Does that mean even the Wraiths are lead within themselves and they will end up facing Albagoth at the end of their days?" Sarah glanced from the Sage to her birth father, Albaohman Davineh.

"Yes, that is true," they both answered her.

"Preposterous!" roared Ira. "When I allegedly died, I never went to Albagoth!" he cleared his throat, "I mean the Nameless One! He never once came down here to claim Marshall and me as his children! I never once felt that entity's presence in my life! I forbid any of my followers from even recognizing him!"

Sarah looked hard at Ira. Pursing her lips together, she walked up to him, put one hand on his heart, and lifted the symbol with her other hand. She placed the symbol to his forehead, "Albagoth is genderless, Ira. Feel Albagoth's presence right now."

Ira's eyes closed involuntarily as his breathing stopped suddenly and he fell into his brother's arms. Marshall laid him down.

The group gasped together.

"Don't worry. He's fine," Sage said. He turned to Sarah, "Do you know what to do now?"

"I'm not sure," she replied slowly. "I can wing it. The words will come to me."

"Let's all go." Sage fixed his vortex manipulator. "Marshall, hold on to Ira so he goes with us."

The group held hands, Sarah took Marshall's free hand.

Xander wondered were Milo was, but before he could say anything, they were whisked away.

Chapter 16

Ira glanced around him. Total blackness. His heart raced and blood flooded in his ears as if he was going through an underground passage. Frantically looking all around him, he wondered where he was and what happened.

"Calm down, my child. All is well," a voice that was neither male nor female said.

"Who speaks to me?" Ira shouted.

"No need to shout," the voice said. "I am the one you deny. I am the one you claim begat you."

"The Nameless One?" Ira said, stunned. "Show yourself!"

Albagoth slowly materialized in the shape of a tree. An old Oak tree. Ira recognized it. It was a tree he used to climb when he was a boy. The tree that used to whisper to him until his mom told him trees couldn't speak to him.

"I" Ira gulped. "You're a tree. Why are you are a tree? How can a tree be a creator?"

"Creators can be anything," Albagoth replied. "I have created many worlds, Ira. I allow you and your brother to find your own path knowing each of your followers will find their way to me once they learn the secrets of going within themselves in meditation. Destroying the Murdocs will not end anyone not uniting with me at their end. Each spirit will return to me."

Ira's spun around and around. Remembering Sage teaching him to breath out his anxiety, he did, expelling the overwhelming elements. Glancing around him, then looking at the tree again, he noticed it changed shape now.

"Who's my father if you aren't?" Ira said. Mystified, he watched the genderless spirit change shape once more to the Sage of Stillness.

"Tomás?" Ira exclaimed. "Why did you change your name to the Sage of Stillness?"

"I am Albagoth in the form of Tomás. Once Tomás finished his spiritual training on all the major worlds he traveled to, he chose to meet with me for further instruction. He said his choices changed. He had twin boys and needed to be close to them. I instructed him what his choices were if he chose to stay on Wayla, admitting he was their father and helping Miriam to raise you two. I showed him what he was giving up and he was okay with it. Your mother did not want him to give up his spiritual guidance of other travelers. He saw the future – he saw Sarah being born. He saw what would happen if you and Marshall continued teaching your beliefs and renouncing the Murdocs. Only Marshall was to acknowledge Sarah's role.

"Tomás chose the name Sage of Stillness so others would know to find the path that is right for them, they had to still their mind. You remained a slave to your own goals and lived the anger and resentment your mother nursed within you. The resentment your mother repented from and tried to undo the day your brother was put to death on the tree. The same tree that Xander Veh, one of my chosen Indigo Travelers, to be tied to later."

Albagoth changed shape again, forming into Ira's doppelganger. "Has anyone told you that you resemble Tomás? You have his coloring, and his nose."

"If I have his nose, I better give it back," Ira said, not intending to be funny. He glanced down. Then back up, "Where am I?"

"You are in the region of space that some of my worlds call the Astroplane. It's place that hasn't been given a name." Albagoth smiled. "Ira, before I send you back to your body, I offer you a choice. Your time as a god on your world is coming to an end. Your followers no longer adhere to your teachings. They refuse to acknowledge you as a living deity. You chose going back and helping Sarah unite the different paths, knowing what she will be teaching them is that all paths are equal. And it is okay to follow their own way if it helps them to grow. Or to allow your body to die right now."

"If I chose to allow my body to die, then what happens to my spirit?"

"It will be sent to the Library of Records to learn more about who you are as a spiritual individual. And review other lives."

Ira welcomed that idea. "I can't live forever?"

"No, you can't. You and Marshall have outlived your bodies. That is was granted you two solely for the lessons you two had to learn and for the lessons you taught others. Now it is time to let go and allow your followers to choose for themselves."

Ira turned around. He wondered if he could see Wayla from here. Gradually, he saw dots of light winking and sparkling. "Stars. There's stars down there. They are so bright and beautiful. I never noticed them before now."

"There will be a lot of things that will look different to you now," the genderless one replied. "What is your choice?"

"I better go help Sarah." Ira turned to face himself. "Albagoth, I'm sorry to be so angry with you all these years. I have noticed Tomás looked like me. I just never wanted to admit it. I explained it away. Now where do I go from here?"

Albagoth's form swirled into a cloud that formed a face. That face took a deep intake of breath and blew it out, blowing Ira's spirit away. "Back to your body."

Ira awoke sitting down in the front of other Wraiths, with Marshall on another path near him. He tried to stand, but his brother turned around and rushed to his side.

Marshall stooped down, "Careful, brother. Ease up. We'll get you some water soon."

Chapter 17

After Ira lost consciousness, the crowd uttered a collective gasped, wondering what happened. Sarah turned over the symbol in her hands, as if in a trance, not sure what to make of what just happened. She brought it up to her forehead, visualizing it growing smaller and pressed it there. Nickoli came up to her side, whispered, "That's one way to get your engraving, but not the traditionally how it happens."

Sarah didn't acknowledge his words. The village square began to spin slowly, gradually picking up speed. Closing her eyes, she eyes, she saw the Wraiths on one path, herself and Nickoli standing in the middle, Sage and all the Albaohmen standing around the inner circle, the Fallen Saviors on a different path and the Murdocs on the third.

When the village square stopped spinning, everyone found themselves standing inside the large symbol on the paths she had visualized.

Marshall laid Ira's body with the Wraiths.

Xander, Geoffrey and Lynx were on the fourth path on the other side of Sarah. Milo appeared soon after, next to them.

Sarah shook her head, not sure what to do now. Nickoli spoke, "Tell them to look at where they are and explain to them what the lines mean. Remember the prayer the Sage said when you, Petra and Jacca were in the cage in the Wraith village."

Sarah bowed her head, closing her eyes, she centered herself, asking Albagoth for assistance. A small voice within her said focus on her gut region, and to utter the words that feel right, acknowledging Albagoth as the center of all paths.

"But I'm not Albagoth. I'm standing where Albagoth is supposed to be," she replied under her breath. The answer came not to worry about that. For now, she was the one standing in the Spirit's place.

"What's this thing called?" Razbuator called out, sneering. "And why are you standing in the middle of it?"

"Yeah, why? Our Fallen Savior should be there! Not you! You're not even from Wayla!"

"Yeah! Our Wraith should be there!" said another Wraith follower.

"No! Our Fallen Savior! He's died for our transgressions when we followed those awful Murdocs!"

"I did not die for your sins! You all made them up after I ascended into the Records Library!" Marshall yelled back. "You all need to stop building on to the story as I lived it!"

"Records Library? You saw the Records library?" Ira's eyes grew large. "I was told I wouldn't see it until after this body died."

Marshall let out a frustrated laugh. "I was dead. But chose to come back to oversee this world and keep you out of mischief. You should have been named Loki."

"Mariam thought of that," Sage Tomás said. "Her parents talked her out of it."

Sarah listened to all the fighting, her own thoughts spinning and as well as an urgency to speak her worlds before everyone started throwing punches at each other.

"Hey, Sarah, may I move?" Xander asked. "I have a suggestion, but I want to whisper it in your ear." She motioned for him to approach her. "Whistle."

Milo said, "Wish for a crow judge."

"No! Crow Judges don't have jurisdiction on Wayla," Sarah answered him.

Sarah nodded. Inserting two fingers in her mouth, taking a deep breath and letting it out, a high, sharp sound pierced the conversations halting the arguments. Everyone looked at her. Xander self-consciously went back to where he was placed. Everyone looked at her.

Sarah sighed, as she considered what to say. She brushed her blond hair away from her face, wishing she had a tie to keep it behind her. Glancing down at her black shirt and crumpled Tripp pants, she realized how long it's been since she'd had a bath and changed her clothes. She wished she could take a shower and put on fresh black clothes. Instead, she just brushed them off, took another deep breath and started talking, not sure what would come out.

"Now that I have your attention, I want you all to notice where you're standing," before she could finish everyone started talking at once again.

"Quiet!" Sage and Manx said loudly. "Allow Princess Sarah to finish!"

Sarah cleared her throat. "Okay, that was a stupid thing to say. You all already see where you are placed. Notice all the paths lead to the inner circle."

"And you have that same symbol on your forehead! That's stupid!" One of the Wraith's yelled.

"I am the uniter of this world! I will bring you all together. I do not call you to change your beliefs but to realize that a proper spiritual teaching will bring your closer to your inner being. That inner being, or spirit is part of Albagoth. This inner circle represents Albagoth, the genderless creator of all Worlds."

"We don't want to be united," the Wraiths and the Fallen Saviors cried. "We want to be separate and kill all Murdocs! We don't want to be like them at all!" Razbuator shouted.

"Yes, we don't want to like them! They threaten us with their peacefulness. They don't ask us to join them. But we want them to convert to our way because we're superior to them!" replied the Fallen Savior leader.

"How are they threatening you if they are peaceful?" Sarah asked.

The Wraiths and the Fallen Saviors looked at each other, each individual searched for how to answer.

Sarah quieted her own anxiety once again, wondering how to lead them. Nickoli tapped her on the leg and she looked down. "Have them walk forward. Tell them to close their eyes and walk towards us, trust yourself and Albagoth to bring about the right message they need to hear and feel within their being."

"But will each of this crowd be whisked away for a face to face with Albagoth?" Sarah asked.

"I don't know. I've never seen Albagoth face to face. Only in visions," Nickoli answered.

"Really? You must tell me about those."

"Not now. Quiet them, Sarah. Have them tune into their inner voice."

She nodded. "Let go of all anguish and thoughts. Listen quietly to my voice. Imagine your thoughts floating away like the dry leaves that are ready to fall off the trees."

She scanned the group, turning around to each group to make sure they were relaxing and listening to her. "Now slowly walk forward towards the center. Imagine the center being what deity you chose it to be."

Sarah felt herself floating up, light like a feather, strong wind blowing her, she allowed herself to be carried away. Gradually a warmth of great love entered her head, gradually traveling down her body. *Well done, my love one,* a voice said inside her being. *Albagoth? She answered. Yes, my daughter.*

Gradually, Sarah was put down next to the Murdocs. She opened her eyes to see she Albaohman Davineh, her biological father, standing beside her, smiling. Pointing towards the inner circle, he whispered, "Look."

Inside the inner circle all the residents of Wayla were standing there, eyes still closed. Reaching out to each other. Murdocs, Wraiths, Fallen Saviors, Xander, Milo, Lynx, Manx and everyone.

"Hug your neighbor," Sarah said.

Sarah's eyes grew wide as she saw everyone meld into one body, love and glowing through love and wholeness. A golden energy mixed with greens, yellows and various shades of blue and deep purple surrounded them. A voice said this how it feels to be reunited with Albagoth, the Creator of all Worlds.

"Why aren't you in the inner circle with the other Murdocs and Albaohmen?" Sarah whispered to her biological father.

"Because my inner voice told me to stand back and watch you. I already knew where I belonged. I am at peace with all."

"Ah" Sarah nodded, but not sure if it was true. His words didn't ring true. She couldn't put her finger on it.

As she looked back, she could see each person begin to redefine themselves. She could see the black robed Wraiths, the orange and yellow robes of the Fallen Saviors and the beige tunics of the Murdocs. Though some of the taller people had to stoop a bit to embrace the smaller pure blooded Murdocs.

"Walk forward, Sarah," Nickoli suggested. She did.

She walked in and among the group, amazed at how each Wraith follower embraced a Murdoc without knowing who it was. And the Murdocs embraced the Fallen Saviors. No fighting, no worries.

"Stand still, let go of the person you're holding. Keep your eyes closed. Imagine the person you were holding, and greeting is your deity. Or a part of you. Love that person and know that person accepts you the way you are.

And you accept that person the way he or she is. Neither one of you want to change the other person."

The atmosphere changed. Sarah sensed the great love she felt within her grow outside of herself and settle on those in the center.

"Open your eyes," Sarah instructed. "Look at who is next to you."

There were gasps, surprised murmuring and disbelief. "If you all remember the paths you were on, go back to those. Stay within your village groups," Sarah instructed.

They did.

The clouds came in, threatening to rain or acidic glass. Marshall and Ira looked at each, winked, clapped their hands and it cleared up.

"We call an end to our mother's acid tears. We will work with our villages to help them build a strong spiritual faith and teach them what we have learned," Ira said. "I chose to bury my anger. The Murdocs were my Mother's people and never threw her out. She left on her own accord."

Sage Tomás agreed. "Who is your real father, Ira?"

"You are. And you always were there for Marshall and me even though you traveled a lot and never came out to admit it. You still helped mom raise us," Ira said.

"What changed?" Sarah asked.

"I had visit with the nameless one – I mean – Albagoth," Ira's face flushed quickly and then vanished.

The Wraiths looked at each other and then the Murdocs.

"What do we do now?" someone asked.

"Let's have a feast," the Albaohmen suggested. "Come to our village and you all can help us make the feast. We can break out the mead and enjoy each other's company."

As they walked back, Sarah heard someone ask a Murdoc guard, "Aren't you all upset that we slaughtered your children, Anansis and caregivers?"

"No, we know they weren't afraid to die and many knew what was coming. Besides, not all the children were killed. Some of them were hidden within Shashamé in the cave. They are on their way back here now."

Sarah was amazed.

She looked at her traveling companions, "Now what?"

"We can go home," Xander said.

"I'm hungry," Milo said.

"Let's stay. I need to talk with my birth father," Sarah said. They nodded, and she went off.

Xander looked at Milo, "Where were you?"

"I had to go off by myself to think. You said you knew for certain your mom found my parents, right?"

"Well, I think so. Clarence came to me in a dream."

"Do you think your Mom will allow me to stay with you all? I want to finish school. And," Milo fidgeted with his hair, and kicked at the dirt. "I remembered that my parents don't accept me because of my gift of granting wishes. They're afraid of touching me."

"And my mom accepts you as you are," Xander said.

"Yes, she does. I can't change who I am for my parents. But I can keep my gift in check during cheer practice and games. I know how to control it."

"I know you do, brother. I'm going to suggest my parents adopt you. I want you to stay with us." Xander slapped Milo on the back. They ran to catch up with everyone else.

Before the feast was prepared, everyone worked together to gather the slain Anansis, Murdoc caregivers and what children they found and buried them. The Albaohmen said prayers releasing the spirits back to the Creative force that their souls came from and asking for their renewed lives on the other side to be fruitful.

The Wraiths and Fallen Saviors spoke of their experience in the middle of the symbol. Each spoke of an immense love like they had never felt before.

Chapter 18

The next day, Sarah and Albaohman Davineh walked on the beach. Sarah scanned the sky, watching the sea birds glide on the light breeze and listening to the peaceful sound as they called to each other. A deep love for the ocean grew in her as she longed to go to the coastal states back home to see how it would be differ from Wayla's coastal area.

Davineh nudged her, startling her. "You're so far away. What are you thinking?"

"I miss my home world. The home you sent me to supposedly keep me safe. Now that I'm here, I feel strange. If I was born here – and this does feel like home – but it isn't my home. You fathered me, yet we hardly know each other. I wonder why or how you could have given me up? And where is my birth mother? Your wife and the queen?"

"You're angry?" Davineh asked.

Sarah nodded yes, then no and shrugged. "I don't know what I'm feeling, Albaohman." She reflected on her words and wondered how to put it all together. "Last night, after I went to bed, I knew what I wanted to say. Nickoli and I discussed it. But now I can't remember anything I wanted to say."

"You lost your nerve. You're afraid of hurting my feelings, so you won't say it out loud," The petite man stopped. "Sarah, look at me."

Sarah turned to look at him, noticing for the first time that his eyes were a deep, dark green, like the sea water. Her insides were stormy like the waters as a storm builds up. Looking into the calm, gentleness of her birth father settled down her turmoil.

"You asked about your birth mom. She is much closer to you than you realize."

"I don't see how," Sarah fumed, stuffing her hands in the deep pockets of her Tripp pants. "I don't see her here and I don't see her back home . . ."

"Sarah," Davineh's soft tone startled her. "Is there someone back home that always shows up when you're upset and you can't get over to Xander's house to talk with him and Milo?"

Sarah shook her head, then thought back. Sighing. She remembered one neighbor who usually appeared to be watching out of her. She was friendly, but her parents seldom saw or noticed her. She was small and had strange ears, like Sarah's, but her mom dismissed that, saying each person has ears that are strange looking.

"There is one person. She told me to call her Queenie. I never thought of that before." Sarah's eyes grew large. "I remember once, when Mom and Dad took Jarrod, Suzie and my other brother somewhere, they left me home. Queenie stayed with me. She told me stories about a land with a fallen savior who loved the forbidden little people who rode spiders. She spoke of that land as magical and the evil dark wizards who threatened to destroy all the trees, spiders and little people because they were angry their fathers denied them love. I remember wanting to visit that land and help the little people. I never thought that the little people literal. Or that I really would be here to unite you all." Sarah looked at him. "Queenie disappeared after I reached my teen years. What happened to her?"

"Queenie was your mother, Sarah. She is still watching over you, but your adopted mom did pay more attention to you than you realized. She's the one that had your birth mom babysit you. When your adopted mom found out Queenie was telling those stories, she grew afraid she would lose you to Wayla once you returned here. Your birth mother is still on the World of Nampa, though. She is not allowed to be close to you. Now that the unity has been established, she will return here."

"Will you and Queenie re-establish the reign? I mean, I am the lost princess, but there isn't a kingdom here in the village anymore."

"You are the found princess. We will still rule, but very different than before. We were never a monarchy that had the royal family sitting above the common folk. We all work together and solve our problems together. Our function more is to settle disputes and make sure the sick and those having a hard time managing their crops get the help they need. With our unity with their villages now, we will establish ambassadors to reach out to them, helping them in any way we can, while making sure they don't have to follow Albagoth in the same way we do.

"Now, Sarah, you have a choice. Are you going to stay here after your coronation?"

Sarah took a deep breath and let it out slowly, turning half way around. Narrowing her eyes, she considered his words. The tide came in, crashing along the shore, spraying her face a bit, refreshing her mind and body. As it ebbed out again, with a swoosh, she wondered where the water goddess was and how she fit into the scheme of this world. Did she play a part in any of them activities? The clouds drifted over the sun, causing a bit of a shadow to grow near them.

"Your mind is a far away again. You likely miss your adopted home world," Davineh said, scratching his chin.

Sarah looked back. "I'm a freshman this year in Columbia High School. I want to finish school. The world you and Queenie agreed for me to be is the only world I know. I have friends there." Those words replayed in her mind, they sounded empty and cold. "I mean, I made some friends here. I know I could learn to adjust to life here. It just isn't what I'm used to. You all don't have technology." She pulled out her cell phone to check the messages. There were no signals.

Davineh cocked his head, "What's that object?"

"It's a cell phone. We use it to call each other or we write messages on it. It's called texting. I brought it with us because I thought I could use it to in case we encounter people who spoke a different language than us. It turns out, it's just a paperweight." Sarah clicked the phone off, taking a deep breath and letting it out, missing the ringing of the message in her in box. "My parents are probably worried sick about me."

Davineh smiled, shook his head. "No, Sage Tomás knows how to manipulate the portals and time streams so you all can be back the day after you left. Or even the day you left Curá. Were you planning to keep Geoffrey with you?"

"Well, he will want to stay with Xander. But it will be hard to hide a griffin. And my big brother wants to kill him. So, we have to find a way to protect him."

"That can be arranged, too. Sarah, are we good? Do you understand more about why we had to give you up and hide you?" Davineh asked, patting her shoulder.

"Yes, I suppose so. In case you're wondering, I'm not angry with you. I was at first. And I will come back to visit. I hope there is a way for us to stay in touch with each other."

After ten to fifteen minutes went by, they heard a splash. Looking out, they saw a large wave come in, go down and part of it rose up with the call, "Shashamé. Shashamé. Albaohman Davineh, the once king will be king again. Indigo Traveler Sarah, the lost Murdoc Princess found, will reign from afar. Come to me to me."

Shashamé rose out of the wave.

"We don't have to come to you water to speak with you, Shashamé. We can speak where we are," Davineh called to her. "We can't stay long. We have a village full of visitors to address and a coronation to plan."

Shashamé's mouth flew open and a loud sound like water being sucked down a drain echoed through the sea scape. A water bird got sucked down her throat, causing her to start choking as she coughed it back up.

"No one! But no one speaks me to like that!" the water goddess barked after she got her words back.

"You do now. Besides, as you already stated, I will be taking my throne again soon. You, as a respected prophet and guide to those who travel through will be limited. I have it on reliable knowledge that you sometimes guide people wrong. Weren't you the one that encouraged Ira to persist in his false belief that Albagoth was his father? Especially when you knew Tomás was?"

"Well – that was a long time ago, Albaohman. I really cannot remember," the water goddess sunk a little bit down.

"Despite Miriam, my great-great aunt, coming to you, urging you to call him back and urge him to face the truth. You couldn't. You will be held accountable."

Shashamé shook her head, "Noo! Nooo, you can't do that! I was only acting on his soul's calling. He had to follow his own inner drive. He had to find out for himself. Explore and know –"

"Yes and no. We encourage those to go within themselves to find their truth, but you didn't speak to him about that. Reason, Shashamé. He followed that inner voice without considering reason and what was in front of himself. You encourage others to go within."

"I do and try to abide . . ." her voice trailed off. Three sea birds flew through her waters, playing tag with the spray that came down like a fountain which formed her hair. She lifted an arm, water dripping down it, to shoo them away. One of the birds snapped at her as if to say she isn't their boss. "Ira was different because he knew what he knew and no one could tell him different. I don't have the luxury of getting out of this water dwelling to commune with a tree."

"Don't you have water trees down there?" Sarah inquired.

"Yes, but they don't respond to me. They respond to the other sea life."

"You're forgiven, Shashamé. We must go. I hope you don't have anything else to say to us," the Albaohman stated.

"No. I bide you two to go with Albagoth. And Sarah, make sure to take Nickoli back to your world. Another traveler will be coming near that need yours and Nickoli's guidance."

"I plan to. Thank you."

They turned around and walked back towards the tunnel to the Murdoc village.

"How is Shashamé related to all this world?" Sarah asked.

"She came with this world. No one knows how she came to be. We all know she does work with Albagoth in some form. Trees try to avoid her waters, though. We have a theory she is quite lonely and is a part siren because there are those she does purposely mislead. And others she doesn't. We can't say for sure."

"Perhaps Albagoth created her like everyone else," Sarah replied.

Xander, Geoffrey, Milo and Sarah gathered outside the meeting hall discussing what would happen next. Sarah, butterflies flitting up and down in her stomach, glanced around at the busy Murdocs preparing for yet another feast.

"We will be having the coronation soon. I've been measured, bathed and scrubbed from head to toe. I've told them they will not dress me in a frilly tunic and no bows or pinks. They didn't understand what I was talking about," Sarah told them.

"Of course not, Sarah. The women here dress like the men and they do the same work. Have you noticed the muscles on the women? They have more women guards and soldiers than men," Milo replied.

"I noticed that," Xander said.

"The only difference is that I will be having Banyan tree branches weaved throughout my blond locks and my hair will be weaved in such a way that it will be a crown. The branches will be woven into the weave, I think," Sarah added. "And my birth father will be having his chosen meditation tree branches weaved throughout his hair, too, to form a crown."

"When are we leaving?" Milo asked. "I'm sure I'm missing cheer practice."

"We'll leave tomorrow," Sarah said. She turned to Geoffrey as Lynx walked up to them. "Geoffrey, do you want to stay with Xander?"

"Yes, that's the plan I had when we left Curá," Geoffrey replied, pawing the ground.

"Great. Sage Tomás agreed to help me put a glamor incantation on you so people who don't know you see you as a large dog."

"Like a Great Dane?" Xander asked. "I've always wanted a Great Dane."

"Yes. Or a Mastiff," Sarah suggested.

"Either will be good," Milo and Xander said together.

"Can I go home with you all?" Lynx asked.

"I'm not sure Clarence would like that," Xander said slowly.

"Yes, we would love to have you!" Milo replied. "Clarence will learn to accept him. It might take some time, but he may enjoy having another companion."

"Two companions. I will be there. Only, Clarence already accepts me," Geoffrey puffed out his albino chest.

"The brave and the proud fall mighty hard," Lynx sneered.

"Smite!" Geoffrey picked up with the claws extended and playful took a swipe at the were-cat.

"Jealous much?" Milo chimed in playfully.

"Quiet from the pea galley," Lynx pouted, drawing down his eyebrows and laying down his ears.

The three Indigo Travelers laughed.

Sarah gathered in the back of the meeting hall to discuss the ceremony. The Anansi spinners and tunic designers dressed. Sarah engraving was woven onto the side of her tunic. Nickoli was also outfitted with a special drape with the path symbol on it. All gathered to see the ceremony.

As Davineh walked down the aisle, he was joined by a Murdoc women Sarah hadn't seen in ages. She aged gracefully yet appeared different than she remembered. Queenie had long Burnette hair and now she had blond hair streaked with black with birch branches woven in it.

"Queenie?" Sarah muttered.

The woman smiled at her. "I'm your birth mother, Sarah. Now that all the paths are at peace, I can come back to Wayla and be with my husband. Won't you stay?"

"I-I," she stared at the ground, "I can't. My life is back in Nampa. I told Davineh that I would visit on Holidays."

"I'm sorry to hear that," Queenie looked at her husband.

After the ceremony, they feasted on sea oysters, trout, rabbit and steamed root vegetables, zucchini and fresh pie made from the sweet cocoa leaves that Queenie brought back from her adopted world.

The next day, the Indigo travelers gathered with Sage Tomás, Marshall and Ira. Sage went through the incantation with Sarah as they stood over Geoffrey.

"Geoffrey, do you know what either of those dog breeds look like?" Sage asked.

"No. I've only briefly been on Xander's world. The first time, I was in cased in stone and the second time, I stayed close to his house. Do I need to know what they look like?" Geoffrey replied.

"Maybe we can shape the spell so each individual will see something different," Sarah suggested, absentminded petting Lynx's head and scratching his ears as he sat beside her.

Manx glanced up at his friend, "That is good idea, Tomás"

Sage nodded. Closing his eyes, he instructed Sarah to do the same. "The purpose of this is to disguise our friend, Geoffrey, so no mere human can see his true form. Sarah, hold out your hand and repeat the words."

Sage uttered, "Grif-fia, prota tria nas-formia canine una Dane largo."

Sarah repeated each word as best she could.

Geoffrey stretched out his wings and flapped afterwards. "I don't feel any different."

"You won't. The only people to see your true form will be those with the second sight and other Indigo teens," Sage said.

"There's more of us?" Milo asked.

"Oh, yes. You might not meet them all. But your world has a lot of teens who feel lost, alone and misunderstood.

Some will spot you three and be drawn to you. Help them out. Not all will be called to journey to other worlds, like you three. Some will travel to alternate dimensions. Guide those teens that come to you," Marshall said.

Others in the Murdoc village gathered around as the three teens gathered their packs and bide everyone good-bye. They climbed on Geoffrey, Lynx, too, who shifted into a smaller cat shape, so he could fit snug between Milo and Geoffrey's neck. Nickoli attached himself to Sarah's back securely so he wouldn't be blown off as they flew

"I'll use my wish gift to make sure we will get through the right worm hole," Milo commented as the albino griffin jumped in the air. "And to make sure we get home within three days of when we left."

The setting sun shone beautiful oranges and yellows with light blues when they landed in the Veh's backyard.

Clarence, Xander's white and orange tabby, who had been laying on top of his dog house, jumped off to greet them. He run up to them, jumped up on Xander's lap, rubbed against him, purring, "It's about time you showed up. The Bickfords are still hear. They're anxious to meet Milo."

Milo jumped off, and so did Lynx. "We meant to get back here before they arrived. How much time has gone by?

"You know I can't tell time, Milo. My staff says it's been almost a week," Clarence replied. But then he spotted Lynx. He jumped off, arched his back, and laid his ears back and his fur rose up as he hissed, "What are you doing here? You're a trouble maker!"

"I'm part of this loving family now, pussycat. So deal with it!" Lynx snapped.

Xander, Milo and Sarah laughed, "That's the werecat we know and love."

211

Sarah ran home. The next day, she came back with her big brother, Jarrod, who was hunting Geoffrey before they left.

"I heard you all got a dog. I want to see this puppy. Sarah said he was cute."

Xander took him into the backyard. Geoffrey, with his tongue hanging up the corner of his mouth, came bounding up to the angry young adult. Sarah greeted Geoffrey, seeing his true form, but treating him like the puppy he was disguised as.

"Oh, my! That's is one large dog! I was sure it was the griffin. But I was mistaken. So, now you get to use that old dog house, eh?" Jarrod said in awe. "I'm surprised your parents agreed to this large dog. Especially since you have a cat."

"Correction, they have two cats now," Lynx said as he jumped up on Geoff's back.

Jarrod fainted.

Acknowledgements

Writing the Indigo Travelers and the Lost Murdoc Princess has been a long process. I had a finished draft a year ago, but discovered I had to change the point of view character after talking with cover artist, Cynthia Martinez.

As I wrote Sarah's point of view, I discovered a whole new world. She is one mighty, strong woman who knows what she wants, though sometimes doesn't know how to get it. She has a wealth of knowledge yet to be discovered. Though, it probably won't be shared yet unless she wakes me up in the middle of the night telling me to write another book with her as the central character. Sarah has woken me up before, to yell at me for not bringing Geoffrey home with Xander after I finished the first Indigo Traveler book. So, Geoffrey is now living with the Veh family and I am sure she is happy about that.

I want to thank my son, James, for helping me last summer with the early stages of editing. We had some lively discussions, which helped me to see what I needed to work on and improve upon. I want to thank Samantha Achaia, at Blazing Butterfly, for editing, formatting and interior design. I also want to thank her for the support and positive reviews.

I want to thank all who have had a part to assist me with developing the story, like Robin Connelly, Jeanette Andersen and many more that I haven't named.

Please remember to go to Amazon and leave a review of Indigo Travelers and the Lost Murdoc Princess. Any review is a good review. And be sure to tell your friends to follow the journey.

About the Author

Merri Halma started writing when she was a pre-teen. She always had an active imagination, so writing helped her channel it. She's studied metaphysics and different spiritual paths for over 20 to thirty years. She has a degree in Counseling-Psychology and combines it in her spiritual paths.

She is the author of Indigo Travelers and the Dragon Blood Sword, Book 1, and Indigo Travelers and the Keys to the Shadowlands Book 2.

Coming Soon

Lynx Faces Himself (working title)
Ian Temple and the Wisdom Trees
And
Haunting of Powell Hall, a novella

Sneak Peek at Lynx Faces Himself
(working title)

Prologue

Lynx, grey and black striped werecat, dragged his ragged body through the Senilona desert, replaying the villagers chasing him out with broom sticks, torches and battle axes, threatening to set him on fire after they arrested his friend and caregiver, Alchemist Blacksmith Tarrier, accusing him of being a traitor to the Crown of Kent Kingdom. Lynx paused, his long, usually fluffy, elegant tail held high, drooped down, looking more ragged and fatigued. He lifted his paws, flexing his four toes and new opposable toe on both front paws. He snapped each toe with close enough, against the first toe. He called his opposable toes thumbs. A few of the men grew positioning their torches close to his hind quarters as he ran. Lynx felt the fire lick his fur and skin. Crying out, his mind switched to kitten hood, engulfed in flames as boys laughed and hooted as they retreated away from the ally way.

"One more demon cat torched. Let's find another," he heard a menacing, gravelly voice hiss. The gang following, raised their voices in agreement.

The Lynx self observing this, knew that Kentese villagers didn't say that. That memory belonged to another time long forgotten and buried. The observer withdrew from the scene.

Chapter 1

Mist rose from the ground and, swirling around the yard giving Lynx, a werecat, with black stripes and spots, in the shape of a Maine Coon, an eerie feeling that something wasn't right. While other mists and scents drifted in from the distant mountains that only Lynx would smell. That scent mixed with another from downtown Nampa that other animals and people would smell. When he first smelled that pungent scent. He asked Xander what it was. He said it smelled like burnt peanut butter. Lynx never heard of peanut butter, so he went inside, brought out a jar of the stuff, gave the werecat a taste. Then the teen put a spoonful in an ashtray and set it on fire, so Lynx could compare the smell. Yeah, it was pretty bad. Lynx said it needed to be banned.

His ears rose, tuning in to frequencies most humans couldn't hear. In the far distance, he heard soulful sobbing from some person or animal that sounded like the person lost their only friend. Yet he couldn't recognize the voice or make out what the person or creature was saying between sobs. A vision of a kitten huddled under a blanket somewhere, pulled his heart strings. Yet he couldn't find it. It was too far away.

"Help me! Not demon cat! Just young werecat. Help me!" The small voice whimpered. Lynx shut his mind, refusing to acknowledge it. It wasn't real. He shut it in a in room somewhere deep down inside his mind. It's too scary. Too much pain. Heartache. Not all humans are bad. Can't say it. "It's not me, I can't help you," he muttered to vision and the cry for help.

Clarence, the white and orange tabby cat that also lived in the Veh house, noticed the werecat's odd behavior. He strode over to him.

"What's it?" Clarence asked. Lynx jumped ten feet high, turned in mid-air and landed in front of the cat. Clarence smiled smugly, enjoying frightening the werecat that always put on a brave, proud and larger than life persona.

"I hear someone or something crying from the depths of his soul," Lynx said. Or imagined he said but wasn't sure if he should admit it. Because if he admitted it, and Clarence couldn't hear it, then he would be made fun of. But this World called Nampa was still a foreign world to him. A world he wanted to live in, because Lynx felt a need to explore other places outside of Curá. Away from his protective home. A place where Lynx could pretend to be something he wasn't to those strangers that came to the Veh house. But those who knew him most – well, no one knew him at all. Lynx quivered inside his skin. He couldn't allow anyone to know the real werecat that he was without his phony shapeshift persona. I couldn't allow anyone to see the true form. They'd run in fear of him. Or burn him at the stake. Though, it was tried once before.

"This mist is spooky," Lynx said. "I see images of spirts and hear voices without bodies." Taking a deep breath, and whiff of the air, "And it stinks!"

"All Hallow's Eve is drawing close," Clarence said. "It's the Sugar beat factory that is working overtime. I don't smell anything else."

"All Hallow's Eve? What's that?" Lynx sat down, tried to smooth his fur down with a wet paw.

"It's the time of year that spirits walk at night, calling to others and witches gather in the woods to celebrate their magic, drawing forth the goodness of what they have brought into this year. Humans see the witches as evil and working with the devil." Clarence shrugged. "My staff says the witches aren't evil, but only want to help each other in the world by restoring balance."

"Balance in what?" Lynx asked, glancing around him at the call of a crow cawing above them.

"Balance in nature and in all things. They want to restore the idea that what each person sends out they will get back three-fold." Clarence chuckled as he noticed Lynx was cowering from the various night birds calling and answering each other.

"What has you so jumpy?" the tabby cat finally asked.

"I keep expecting a Crow Judge to come and arrest me for violating some law of Curá that I hadn't heard of." Lynx lowered himself further to the ground. "Then I remember the Crow Judges don't monitor the World of Nampa."

"You aren't as tough as you want others to think you are, werecat," Clarence chided. "Relax. You're too hard on yourself." The tabby stood up, stretching his front legs and then his back legs and started heading for the back porch doggy door. "I'm going in to a warm bed beside Xander."

"You're going to leave me out here to the witches and ghouls?" Lynx cried.

"Yep. Sure am. My dog house is warm. My staff put a warm blanket or two in there this morning."

"Night!" Lynx muttered, glancing around.

Looking up at the round bright orange moon with a white halo around it, Lynx wondered what truly was out there. The moon called him, but he couldn't make out exactly what it was saying to him. It appeared larger than normal. Taking a deep breath and letting it out slowly, he stood up and walked to the dog house and went inside. He picked up a blanket, put it over his shoulder and spread the other one down on the ground and then laid down on it and put the second over his body.

Raising his front paws to his face, he spread his toes out, examining them one by one, meditating on how he could use them to improve his deep fear. Or find who was hurting so bad.

"Albagoth, I'm not sure you answer creatures like me. I feel so a lone and isolated. I -I-I . . ." Lynx paused in mid-sentence. "I don't know what to say."

Clicking his first toe and his thumb together, just to make sure they still worked, he wished to see who was crying and so deeply hurting. He didn't transport anywhere, though. He stayed right where he was. Frustrated, he yawned, turned over on his side. Then decided to curl up like the big kitten he was shaped to be.

***

Mists swirled around him, rising and falling, shaped like humans with wings climbing an invisible ladder while other taunted him. Lynx walked alone in the forest, but he couldn't make out where the trees were and where the body of water was.

"You're lost, Lynx. You're not you who you think you are. Can you even see yourself on a clear day?" One of the beings taunted.

"You're such an ugly creature, your horrible werecat. You know you're ugly, that's why you hide in the shape of a socially acceptable Maine Coon. You're afraid of seeing your true form." Another said.

"Go away! I know who I am! I am who I want to be!" Lynx barked.

"Ooh! A cat who barks commands us to go away. What do you say, gentlemen and gentleladies, should we listen to him? I bet he can't even listen to himself!"

"Yeah!" the chorus agreed. They laughed.

"I thought you were angels! You look more like demons to me!" Lynx said snidely.

"Demons?" another stated.

"Angels?" another asked. They laughed with the group.

As whole, they cried out, "We are neither what you or the humans have created. We are just the ones who poke at those who live in fear. You, Lynx Werecat, are afraid of being yourself!"

A loud, mournful cry pierced the jabs and laughter. Lynx growled and hissed at these horrible creatures, and they finally disappeared. He followed the cry up a long and winding path, which lead up a steep hill. As he neared the top, the mist cleared. The light from the moon shined on one solitary figure curled in a heap of blankets, sobbing and whimpering, "Help me! It hurts! I didn't do anything. Help me, please."

Lynx carefully walked up to the animal, lifted a paw and gently touched it's back.

"What's wrong, friend?" he asked.

The animal stopped sobbing, looked and it bursts into flames. Lynx jumped back, screamed.

Chapter 2

Lynx whimpered loudly, sobbed, "Noo! Noo! Stop! Stinging! I'm innocent! Please stop!" he rolled around, patting himself, twisting the blanket around and around his long, fluffy body until he couldn't move. "Let me go! I'm not a demon! Honest! I'm just a kitten! A baby. Have mercy!"

Mercy is for the beautiful and the confident! came the dream image.

"Lynx! Lynx, wake up!" Geoffrey, the albino Griffin stuck his head in the doghouse. "You're having a nightmare. You're going to wake up the household."

Geoff gently toughed the werecat on the shoulder. Lynx woke up, eyes wide and claws out.

"What?!" He spotted the griffin, relaxed. "Oh, Geoffrey. I'm glad it's you."

"I can hear your heart racing a mile a minute. Sit up and relax. When you're ready, want to come hunt with me? We can talk about your dream."

Lynx sat up, looked down at his stomach. "I'm not sure I want to talk about it. You'll think I'm a wimp."

Geoffrey chuckled, "You're no wimp, Lynx. We all have our weaknesses. I think this world is enough different than the one we came from, that is bring up new fears we both haven't dealt with since we were young. I am there to listen to you when you are ready to discuss what is going on with you, though."

Lynx smiled. "Yeah, I know. Give me a minute. A good hunt might be what I need."

"You have it," the griffin nodded and backed out of the dog house.

Lynx sat up, looked at his front paws, images of his dreams and the charred face he saw frightened him to no end. He shuddered, lowering himself back to the ground and tried to bury his himself under the blankets.

A loud thud shook the large dog house, startling the werecat. Next came claws slowly scrapping along the tile roof. Lynx didn't want to look up or get out even though his stomach growled and rumbled.

"Boo!" Clarence hung his head over the opening.

"EEYeow!" Lynx jumped out from under the covers. Clarence laughed.

www.ingramcontent.com/pod-product-compliance
Lightning Source LLC
Chambersburg PA
CBHW020405150626
46554CB00012B/313